LOST IN AMERICA

A. S. FRENCH

NEONOIR BOOKS

ALSO BY A. S. FRENCH

The Astrid Snow series.

Book one: Don't Fear the Reaper.

Book two: The Killing Moon.

Book three: Lost in America.

The Detective Jen Flowers series.

Book one: The Hashtag Killer.

Book two: Serial Killer.

Book three: Night Killer.

Go to www.andrewsfrench.com for more information.

1   I JUST CAN'T BE HAPPY TODAY

The stare on his face was so hard you could sharpen knives on it. His voice was as thin as the rest of him and seesawed up and down like an out-of-tune violin. Astrid ignored it and considered how she'd ended up inside a jail in small-town America, twitching her nose at the smell of sweat drifting from her. She rubbed at the bruise on her cheek and wriggled her mouth to squeeze out the ache in her jaw.

What is that taste lingering on my lips?

The Police Officer repeated something, but all she heard was last night's terrible band banging the drums inside her ears and that woman screeching through her skull.

I'm the queen of raaack and rollll!

She couldn't get that scream from her head.

She's the one who did this to me.

Astrid licked at the stale tequila squatting at the back of her throat and remembered getting into the fight with the lead singer from that group.

She was no queen of anything, let alone rock-and-roll. Her name was Stella Starr, and the band was London Riot.

She'd pushed her way to the stage, fighting through the rednecks and mullets, and shouted at them. 'You're more like London Shite!'

The tequila missed her mouth and slipped from the bottle, splashing the giant of a bloke swaying next to her. She ignored his scowl and scanned the room: the bar was a mating ground for those whom evolution had forgotten: apish men with shaven heads dragged their knuckles along the floor while lumbering after women in white stilettos and matching PVC catsuits, who clattered around blaring like banshees to match the singer.

As she sat in the police cell, her brain recalled the mixed aromas of the night before: the strong whiff of tobacco and fatty foods with subtle hints of exhaust fumes, sweat and damp vegetables from the market area; all with an undertone of vomit, Hai Karate aftershave and old cheese. The Officer continued to say things she didn't hear as a rush started in her toes and surged up through her body. The memories released thousands of tiny bubbles of booze and chilli into her veins. She felt like a shaken-up bottle of Lucozade as he opened the door and reached for her.

Then she vomited all over him.

His angry shouts loosened the cotton wool in her head as he pushed her back on to the bed. She hit it with a thump and the metal edge bit through her jeans and into her leg. As she rubbed at it, her ribs throbbed to a similarly bruised tune. The policeman pulled away from her and locked the door behind him, retreating down the corridor and filling the air with a choice selection of obscenities.

She rolled on to the bed and gazed at the ceiling. Someone had scrawled pornographic drawings into the concrete, but they didn't distract her from returning to last night's activities. She wasn't in the cell any more, but back in the dive bar, at the front of the stage and harassing the singer. That tall woman, Stella, jumped down to punch her; wasn't that what happened? The memories were fuzzy, but Astrid knew one thing: she was a Brit in an American bar and was in no mood to refuse an international challenge, even though she should have returned to England days ago.

A crude caricature of two policemen having sex brought her back to reality. Astrid wondered if the station's occupants ever looked at the ceiling to see what was there. She wiped the taste of vomit from her lips, but could do nothing about the smell of what she'd drunk last night sticking to the walls of her nose like a thick carpet. She steadied her legs and lurched towards the far wall, amused to notice a map peering at her. She assumed it was of the town, but most of the names printed across the top had faded over the years, so all it read now was B##ERSTOWN. The crick in her neck twitched as she pushed her face close to the text.

Perhaps I'm living in BEERSTOWN. How appropriate would that be?

She rubbed at her rumbling stomach as she examined the figures on the paper. If her current accommodation was a jail in the town's police department, then according to the map, she was bang in Main Street's centre. On her release, she could turn left and pop into the Well-Read bookstore and perhaps pick up a rare copy of *The Bell Jar*. Next door was Tom's Diner, and perhaps they'd have something to quell the grumbling inside her guts. Further on, she'd visit the drug store and the perfume shop, perfect places to ease her aching bones and improve her smell. If she kept going in the same direction, she'd eventually reach Siggy's Used Cars and perhaps use their expertise to get out of this town without relying on the bus service that brought her there.

Her other option would be to turn the opposite way and step into the movie theatre; hadn't she seen an advert somewhere for a revival double feature of *Alien* and *Aliens?* Then again, her memories of last night were few and covered in hazy fuzz, plus the idea of spending so long in the dark didn't appeal to her. In that case, she could visit the town hall on the other side of the road, or possibly find some spiritual redemption inside the United Methodist Church or the First Church of the Baptist; only Main Street separated the two places of worship. That and the religiously themed delicatessen called Jesus Cheeses. Then came the brewery, and beyond that were a hospital and a sign leading off the map, pointing to WORTHING WOODS at the end of the street.

All the town's roads had unassuming names apart from a long, winding one on the east side named DOGS HEAD ROAD. The title intrigued Astrid, and the path led into a swathe of trees surrounding most of the town. She reached out and ran her fingers across the wrinkled paper, the touch of it resurrecting memories of the first maps she'd created in her family home so long ago. The twinge in her brain would soon grow into a roaring locomotive if she didn't get her past under control. She had several mechanisms to deal with this, honed and cultivated over time to near perfection, but they weren't needed now since the soreness in her ribs was making her body flinch and returning her mind to the present.

She stepped back, her leg bumping into the bed as she pulled up her top to stare at the vivid purple and blue imprinted on her skin. Then the memories came, not of her childhood, but of yesterday and the beating she'd taken. She shook her head and gazed at the map, only noticing from that distance someone had drawn on it two stick figures having sex at the bottom of the paper.

If she scrunched up her eyes, they reminded her of ants grappling with each other. This image triggered the flickering frames of her father over thirty years ago, dragging her into the garden to make her watch as he set an ant colony on fire. It wasn't the illumination of the flames or the smell of the smoke which stuck with her the most, but the sight of him, of Lawrence Snow, leading light of the local police force, and the expression of pure joy which lit up his face.

She resurrected the bile at the bottom of her throat because the taste of it was better than thinking about him. Astrid turned towards the bed, noticing for the first time the newspaper underneath it. Her ribs tingled as she reached down and grabbed it. She'd hoped it would be the local rag so she could find out where she was, but it was a two-day-old copy of the *New York Times*. The cover and front pages focused on the President's decision to pull all US troops from the Middle East, talking of a partial withdrawal from Europe to follow. He was a Good Old Boy, and his action against his military advisors' advice was going down well in the Red States. She flicked by the news for a crossword or puzzle to keep her brain active.

'Welcome to American justice.'

The guy who spoke was not the Officer she'd thrown up on. He opened the cell door, swinging keys in one hand and clutching a cup of coffee in the other. It wouldn't have mattered if he'd been cradling two shotguns like an over-excited John Wayne. Even in her present state, she could have dropped him without a second thought. Then it would be a quick walk down to the exit from the cells, through that and past the motley crew of doughnut eaters and moustache groomers she'd staggered by in the early hours of the morning. Even with her Armageddon-inducing headache, it wouldn't be too much of a problem. But what then? Flee from small-town Americana and blag her way back to Blighty? That would only cause more problems.

The guy read Astrid her rights. He had a long, narrow face, with straight angular bones hiding beneath the skin, sharp enough to slice through steel. Frozen eyes sat in two sunken fleshy holes. His short brushed hair sprang forward from the top of the head like the brittle wire on a brush, flecked with white and grey.

'Do you understand what I said, Brit girl?'

She kept her fist from smashing into his nose for calling her a girl. 'I'm guessing my comprehension of the English language is greater than yours, Yank boy.' Astrid placed heavy emphasis on the word Yank. Sweat poured off him like a monsoon. He stank of cheap aftershave and desperation. Wrapped around his face was one of those hipster beards only a jackass would have.

Astrid had travelled through New York State for a week, stopping in a few small towns, tempted to visit Greece in Monroe County because of its name, and then continue to her ultimate destination in Rochester. But she'd needed rest from the beaten-up bus carrying her weary body before she got there and took a break in this one-horse town. The tangle with Stella Starr was the first entertainment she'd had in weeks, and even though her head and ribs throbbed like superheated electricity, she didn't regret it. Whatever this was now, it seemed unlikely to be enjoyable. But she wasn't worried; how long would she be locked up for getting into a fight?

His teeth were un-American in their crooked, nicotine-stained shape. 'You're in deep trouble, girl.'

Astrid had left her teenage years behind a long time ago, so she assumed he was calling her girl to wind her up. Or perhaps his experiences with women were that limited, which, looking at him again, she could well believe.

'Where am I?'

He stared at her as if she was dumb. 'You're in jail, Brit girl.'

There was that word again. She licked the last of the stale tequila from her lips.

'Which village are you the idiot of?'

He had a face designed to sneer. 'Turn around with your hands behind your back.'

She did as instructed and the handcuffs bit into her skin. He didn't waste the opportunity of leaving grubby fingers lingering across the top of her legs. She fought off the urge to kick him in the balls. He spun her around and glared at her, so close she thought the halitosis would melt the flesh from her cheeks.

'You're in Bakerstown, Brit girl, and there's no fancy lords or ladies to get you out of this mess. Even the King of England can't help you now.'

She wondered where he got his curious knowledge of Britain and its residents from as he shoved her towards the exit, then reached above her head to bang on the faded paint of the wood. A sewer lived in his armpit, and she wanted to throw up again. The door opened as she shovelled the bile back down her throat.

She stepped out, keen to get away from the stink surrounding her. A blonde woman stared at her from behind a computer screen. She had fingernails so long, Astrid thought it would be impossible to type with them, but she caressed those keys as if born to it. Stationed across the room were several Officers with guns strapped to their waists, their heads turning towards her in unison.

No American could ever understand how strange it was for a Brit to witness weapons worn so openly and casually. Even with the police, it was a rarity to see that in Britain. She'd had training with firearms, but had never been comfortable around them. She guessed it gave people a sense of security they didn't need in a town this small; then again, perhaps Bakerstown was a lot more dangerous than the name suggested. Why else would they lock her in a cell?

All this because I got into a fight with that woman from the band?

The stink cop shoved her to the left and inside another room, furnished with a single table and three chairs. The walls were as barren as the rest of the building, the carpet stolen from the Ark. Wherever the money was in this town, it wasn't with the local police department.

A camera peered at her from the corner of the ceiling, but nobody had switched it on. The stink cop told her to sit down and removed the handcuffs. Then he left, locking the door with her inside. All she had to do was wait. And that wouldn't be a problem as long as she kept her hyperactive brain satisfied. So she scrutinised the room and contemplated her situation.

She was an expert in seclusion. It was Astrid who'd codified the isolation interrogation process and procedures in her previous employment. Was that what this was about? Did her employers want her back and were they trying the same techniques against her which had failed before?

Perhaps I should be worried about this.

A man unlocked the door and entered with a woman. He looked like a young Denzel Washington but with none of the confidence, and she was a mouse in a dress, all edgy tics and restless eyes. He took Astrid's mug shots, and she did the fingerprints. Astrid was glad it was the woman who got to hold her hands, with the feel of her skin distracting enough to quell the warning signs exploding through her head. The woman was even more nervous after Astrid finished flicking her eyelids at her. They didn't bother to cuff her again before leaving.

She checked the place after they'd gone, staring past the dead camera and the American flag on the wall. A large man shuffled into the room. She wasn't sure how he fitted into the chair opposite her, but he did. The wood creaked so loudly she expected it to shatter at any second.

He sneered at her and spoke through lungs caked with decades of nicotine.

'You're in a lot of trouble, girl.'

She tried not to smile. His face had too much flesh on it, as if bits were trying to find an escape route by swimming through the sweat dripping down his receding hairline and the lakes settling under his eyes.

'Is this how you treat all your guests?'

He ignored her question. 'My name is Colt, Chief of Police in this town you've invaded.' He made it sound as if she was the first wave of a barbarian horde. He threw papers on to the desk, bits of food sticking to his chubby fingers. 'Your visa expired weeks ago, Snow, and the British Embassy in Washington wants nothing to do with you, considering your crimes here. All you can do now is confess to them.'

There was hate in his eyes which stretched further back than whatever she was supposed to have done. She might have a stonewall alibi for what he was about to accuse her of, but it wouldn't make a jot of difference.

I don't have one for that fight.

'My lead Detective will deal with you, but not yet. After what you did, it's gonna be my pleasure to set you on the path to a life in prison.' He rolled his eyes at her. 'Being a Brit ain't gonna help you now, girl; those limey bastards have washed their hands of you. So what do you think of that?'

'What am I supposed to have done?'

He leant back into his chair, and she waited for the snap, which never came. He smoked an imaginary cigar and glared at her. She said nothing, still confident she'd get out of this when she had to, waiting for Colt to tell her.

'You're a murderer, Snow.'

2   GRAVE DISORDER

The words echoed inside her head as Chief Colt banged on the wall behind him. The door creaked open, and a tall man strode inside. He looked like he'd stepped out of a Vietnam movie, with cold sea-blue eyes and a scar on his right cheek. He took the other seat and removed a digital recording device from his pocket. His voice was melodic, like an angel's tears.

'I'm Detective Moore, and I'll be conducting this interview. Do you need a lawyer?' Astrid shook her head. 'You have to say it out loud for the record.'

They stared at her as she considered her options.

'I don't want a lawyer.' She wanted a drink, but none of them had offered her anything. Apart from the lawyer she didn't need.

Moore continued. 'Do you know where your passport is?'

'The last I checked, it was in my pocket before the...'

The Detective inched closer to her. 'Before what?'

Astrid touched the bruises below her shirt. 'Before the fight with the woman in the bar last night.'

He peered at his papers. 'You were in an altercation at the Ranch House shortly before midnight.' It was a statement, not a question.

'With singer from the band, Stella Starr.'

He seemed unimpressed with her local music knowledge. 'What happened between you two?'

Faint shadows lurked inside her brain of another woman and another conflict last night. She scratched at the top of her head, hoping to pick out her missing memories.

'Her band was terrible, and she sang like a demented poltergeist. So I told her.'

Moore skimmed through his notes. 'And she heard you through the noise?'

Astrid rubbed dirt from her fingers. 'I climbed on stage and took the microphone from her. Then I told everyone how shit the group was, especially her.'

His mouth twitched, and she guessed he was fighting a smile.

'I bet that went down well.'

'I don't know; I couldn't hear above the screaming. I jumped down and barged outside. The next thing I know, the demented banshee grabbed me by the neck and threw me to the ground. By the time I'd wiped the crap from my face, the whole of the bar was whooping and hollering as Starr give me a good kicking. You must have witnesses for that.'

'Why didn't you fight back?'

Astrid ran her fingers across her shirt, finding the bruises underneath.

'I probably deserved it.'

'Because of what you did on stage?'

'That and other things.'

Moore returned to his notes. 'Do you remember what happened next?'

She delved into the wreck of her memories and uncovered the ones submerged from last night. Starr scowled at her as the crowd howled for blood, the shouts of USA, USA, cutting through the cold night with every volcanic syllable. Then they left her in the mud and returned indoors for more shit music and weak beer. Everybody abandoned her, but one.

Caitlin Cruz.

'You need patching up.' *She reached down to me.* 'We're not all animals here.'

Astrid stared at Moore. 'Caitlin took me home.'

'We know this.' He fiddled with the papers. 'You were on first-name terms?'

'She was polite.' Astrid pulled up her shirt and touched the bandage around her ribs. 'She tended my wounds and gave me a drink.'

'Is that all?'

She scrutinised his face, knowing there was more, but struggling to recall the events.

'I think we sat awhile and talked, waiting for me to recover before I returned to town.'

Moore scribbled on to his notepad while Chief Colt continued to stare at her.

'What did you talk about?'

She ran a hand through her hair, her fingers scratching along her scalp in an attempt to remember.

Caitlin.

They were on first-name terms as they drank together. She was dressed in jeans and an oversized checked shirt. A light smattering of makeup covered her face, but was not overdone, while her black hair was pulled into a ponytail.

There was something in how Cruz composed herself which confused Astrid, as if she was unsure of where she was. Her gaze moved quickly over everything around her, peering over Astrid's shoulder and through the window.

'We agreed on how shit the band was. She said she'd show me a better bar sometime.'

'Nothing happened between you?'

Her ribs rippled with laughter, and she held back a grimace. 'What do you mean, Detective Moore?'

'When Caitlin patched you up and you talked, where were you in the house?'

She narrowed her eyes, wondering where he was going with this.

'When we got there, she took me into the kitchen. I didn't go anywhere else.'

'Not even upstairs?'

'Nope; only the kitchen.'

'So, nothing physical happened between the two of you?'

Is that what this is about?

'She saw me without my shirt on when she bandaged my ribs, but that was about it.' Astrid smiled at Chief Colt. 'I'm sorry to disappoint you boys, but there was no girl on girl action between Caitlin and me in that house that night.' Colt didn't take his eyes off her. 'And even if it did happen, is that a crime in this town?' She focused on Detective Moore. 'Has Bakerstown retreated to a mythical 1950s when men were men and women did as they were told and everything was whiter than white?'

He ignored her question. 'What happened after she dressed your injuries and your little talk?'

Astrid dug into her brain again like one of those attractions in the amusement arcades where you try to grab a toy using a mechanical digger.

'Caitlin dropped me at the bar a few hours later.'

'Why return there?'

'I had unfinished business with the Poundland Janis Joplin.'

Moore raised his eyebrows. 'What's a Poundland?'

'It's a shop back home where you can buy the cheapest tat you'd ever want.'

'Okay. What did you do when you returned to the bar?'

Astrid pressed her fingers into her damaged ribs. 'It had closed, and the place was empty, so I headed to my hotel. Only I didn't get there.'

'Why?'

'I must have blacked out. Too much booze and a beating can do that to you, Detective. I'm guessing that's when your lot found me.'

'Which is why you're here now.'

'For being drunk and disorderly?'

'No, Ms Snow, for murdering Caitlin Cruz and her two children.'

The pain in her ribs sprinted through the rest of her body with a vengeance. Colt's smile grew so large, she thought it would fall off his face. Moore sat stony-faced.

'That's crazy, Detective.'

'I'm afraid not, Ms Snow.' He didn't look afraid to her. 'You were found passed out near the Ranch House Bar and Grill. Two hours later, you were in a cell here.'

That didn't sound right to Astrid. 'I recollect some of your Officers dragging me here in the middle of the night, on some trumped-up charge of disturbing the peace.'

Moore searched through his paperwork again. 'Things have changed since then, Ms Snow. Officers brought you here at two in the morning.' He looked at his watch. 'It's now five minutes before ten. Forty-five minutes ago, we found your bloodied passport on the body of Caitlin Cruz. How do you think that happened?'

Astrid's mind continued to buzz like a swarm of bees drunk on honey.

'I had my passport with me in the bar. I didn't trust leaving it in that fleabag hotel, so I took it with me. Maybe it fell out of my pocket during the fight. Or perhaps somebody stole it from me there.'

Chief Colt snorted with laughter as Moore's expression remained unchanged.

'Do you think either of those things is possible?'

'Most things are possible, Moore.'

He placed his hands together. 'You believe someone stole your passport from you while you were at the Ranch House?'

She shrugged. 'Maybe.'

Colt didn't contain himself. 'We've read your file, Snow. You used to be some kind of British spy, and now you're claiming a hick inside the bar was good enough to steal your passport without you knowing?'

When he put it like that, it sounded ludicrous. Yet, she couldn't see how it would have happened any other way.

'I was drunk.' The ache in her skull continued to remind her of that. 'Or perhaps one of those hicks kicked it out of me when I was in the dirt.'

Moore regained control of the interview. 'Your passport was discovered on Caitlin Cruz's body, not long after eyewitnesses saw the two of you together after the altercation outside the bar.'

'I told you, she took me to her place to tend to my wounds.'

'Are you sure nothing else happened at the Cruz house apart from what you've told us?'

Was she sure? Things were missing from her memory, she knew that, but murder wasn't one of them. Those redacted parts of her mind from her childhood had been joined by blind spots from last night. She put them down to her tiredness on arrival, too much booze, and the beating she'd taken. And she also realised they'd come back, eventually. But, after looking at Colt and Moore's faces, she wondered if she had the luxury of waiting for them to return.

'I'm sure, Detective.'

The Police Chief grinned at her while Moore seemed disturbed.

'Someone murdered Ms Cruz's children in her house. Their faces were burnt with acid, just like their mother. We discovered your fingerprints in the residence.'

Kids? I didn't see any children there.

'What?'

He played with the paperwork again, shuffling the bits around so she glimpsed what he was scrutinising. Then he removed two photos and placed them in front of her. 'This is what they used to look like. Cathy Cruz was fifteen, her brother, Dale, ten years old.'

Astrid heard his voice, but it was as if the words were echoes vibrating from somewhere far away, drifting in and out of her head like an interrupted radio wave. Her shoulders dropped as she stared at the images of the two murdered kids. Both photographs looked as if they'd come from an official school album: Cathy Cruz had a lop-sided grin which highlighted the braces on her teeth, the pure whiteness of which was in stark contrast to the sky blue of her large eyes. Her dark hair was jet black and hung to her waist. The roundness of her cheeks was replicated in her brother, but his eyes were paler and narrower, his short hair parted on the left and swept from his brow. They appeared as sweet and innocent as she guessed they must have been.

But now they were dead, and the two men sitting opposite believed she was responsible.

'Were all three murdered the same way? Was it the acid that killed them?'

Detective Moore ignored her questions. 'Did you see Cathy and Dale while you were in the house, Ms Snow?'

Had she? She couldn't recollect doing so, but that didn't mean she hadn't. Those blind spots from last night, this morning, were still there, so maybe she did see them.

The killer could have been inside, with the four of us, all the time I was there.

'I don't remember seeing them.'

Moore leant forward. 'But you could have and forgot?' The silent digital recorder seemed to pulse and bleep inside Astrid's head as it recorded everything he said. 'Is it possible you spent time with Cathy and Dale, but you've blanked out the memories?'

She wanted to shout no at him, but didn't, instead arching her back further into the uncomfortable chair. The full enormity of what was happening was only just sinking in.

'While you're wasting time with me, the actual killer is running around somewhere.'

'Do you know who that is?'

Astrid searched through her scrambled skull, sifting out the noise from the bar and the band and the fight. The ache in her ribs throbbed again as she pictured staring into Caitlin Cruz's welcoming face and the hand she held out to her. She took it and let Cruz lead her into the car before they drove to her place. How long was the drive?

That's another missing memory. I drifted in and out of unconsciousness, more because of the booze than the beating.

But she remembered pressing her head up against the window, the icy touch of the glass trying to keep her awake. There were no buildings outside in the gloom, only the countryside passing them by. There was noise on the radio: some music she hadn't heard before. It was low and melancholic, with a woman singer telling a tale of betrayal and deceit.

They arrived in the middle of nowhere, with Astrid unsure how long it had taken to get there. She'd pay more attention on the way back, realising Cruz's place was only twenty minutes from the bar. But before that, she recalled Caitlin leading her into the house and the two of them going into the kitchen. They didn't go through the front, but the rear, up a set of steps and inside.

The door wasn't locked. Cruz just pushed it open and took me in.

So anybody could have been waiting for them. As that possibility stabbed at her heart, Detective Moore repeated his question.

'Do you know who murdered Caitlin, Cathy and Dale Cruz, Ms Snow?'

Astrid shook a single word from her mouth. 'No.'

'Did you see Cathy and Dale Cruz in the house, Ms Snow?'

'No.'

'Did you see the children outside the house, front or back, Ms Snow?'

'No.' She would have remembered seeing two kids there.

Wouldn't I?

'Did you go upstairs, Ms Snow?'

'No.'

'But the kids could have been there, and you wouldn't have known it?'

'Of course. It was late, so I'd expect kids to be asleep then.'

'What time did you get to the Cruz house?'

Astrid had a good idea of that. The band came on stage at nine and were near the end of their ninety-minute set when she harassed them. That meant she was getting a kicking outside the bar at about ten forty-five. If that were over by eleven, she would have been inside the Cruz kitchen around thirty minutes later.

'About eleven-thirty.'

As she answered his questions, Moore continued making notes. Chief Colt sat and picked at his teeth, with his unflinching gaze fixed on her throughout the interview. Then the Detective surprised her by changing tack.

'Your passport is British, but where are you from, Snow? What's your background?'

Astrid sucked in the air as if it was a three-course meal and she hadn't eaten for days. Whatever this nonsense was, she wasn't getting away from it soon.

Don't volunteer any information you shouldn't.

That's what they'd instructed her at the Agency. But now she felt like talking.

'I was born in a small village in the north of England, which you've probably never heard of. My mother was a teacher, my father, a copper.'

Moore stopped making notes and stared at her. 'He's retired?'

'You could say that.' Most people lose their jobs when

they're discovered hurting one of their kids, even a high-ranking Police Officer. 'I have an older sister who hates me.'

'Why does she hate you?'

'It's complicated.' Made more so by the niece she loved who could have died because of her. 'I ran away from home, hooked up with a gang, nearly went to prison but was rescued by a socially conscious group of adults.'

Moore raised his eyebrows. 'Who were these people who helped you?'

'They're a charity organisation.'

They were a clandestine government intelligence outfit called the Agency.

'Why did you come to the US?'

This was the tricky part. 'I wanted to see the sights. Then I forgot about the date on my visa.'

She'd come to return a kidnapped kid to her mother in England before getting talked into another rescue mission in the States. But she still couldn't work out why she hadn't returned home yet.

Perhaps it's because I don't have a home.

'Why haven't you left?'

'It's a big country, Moore; there's lots more to see.'

He put his pen down. 'Why did you kill the kids? Starr beat you badly in front of dozens of people, which must have wounded your pride and your body. Then Caitlin Cruz played the Good Samaritan and took you home to sort out your injuries. Perhaps in your pain and embarrassment, you lashed out at her, looking for revenge on Starr. I guess that's possible, I get that, but you didn't have to hurt those children.'

Astrid shook her head. What he claimed to have was circumstantial, but he and his cronies could drag it out forever. If the authorities were that incompetent or corrupt, it might even make it to court. She let out a long, irritating groan.

'This is pointless.'

Moore curled his lips in satisfaction. 'Have you realised the seriousness of the situation?'

Astrid grimaced at him. 'No, but I might have to contact some people I don't want to. Am I allowed one phone call?'

'Sure, but before that, would you tell me why you ended up in this town?'

She racked her mind for the answer, pushing past the alcohol, the bruises and the frustration.

'I was on my way to see a grave.'

3 LITTLE MISS DISASTER

Colt stuck out his ample belly and laughed at her. 'Were you visiting someone else you killed?'

She peered deep into his frog-like eyes and wondered how many kids he'd eaten for breakfast.

'I'm passing through Bakerstown on the way to Rochester. Somebody famous is buried there.'

She didn't know why she told them that, assuming the irritation in her ribs would soon spread through her blood and bones until it banged on her brain and she couldn't handle it any longer. Perhaps she should take up the offer of a lawyer after all.

Chief Colt tipped his hat at her. 'I doubt you'll be seeing Rochester or anywhere else for a long time, lady.'

At least he didn't call her a girl. 'Is that all you have: a few eyewitnesses who saw me leave with Cruz and my passport found on her body?'

Colt nearly fell from his chair as he snorted with laughter. 'That'll be enough for a jury here, Miz Snow. And even if it wasn't, your prints and DNA are all over the Cruz house, plus we know how foul your mood was in the bar. And how drunk you were.'

She smiled at him. 'That's not true, though, is it?'

His grin was wide enough to swallow her whole. 'Which part?'

'The bit about my prints and DNA being all over the house. I never left the kitchen; apart from Caitlin's car, it's the only place you'll find any evidence of me. And I told you more than once how and why I was there.'

Detective Moore continued. 'But your passport was found inside Caitlin Cruz's pocket, with both of your blood on it.'

He peered straight into her, a slightly unnerving gaze which she guessed meant the passport had convinced him of her guilt. But then he let his eyes linger on her for a second too long, and she thought she glimpsed something else behind his scrutiny; some little sliver of doubt.

Colt grasped his hands together like Scrooge in a bank vault, and she considered what her next move should be. She ignored him and spoke to Moore.

'What motive would I have for killing them?'

'Anger, frustration, too much alcohol in your veins.'

She shook her head. 'They're excuses, not motivation.'

'Perhaps Cruz resisted your advances, Snow, and then you lashed out at her.' She watched as Colt laid out his theory, something she guessed he'd been formulating before meeting her for the first time. 'With your training and expe-rience as a covert intelligence agent for the British govern-ment, you'd have been well prepared to overpower her. And the children, poor Cathy and Dale, saw the whole thing, so you couldn't leave them alive.' His self-satisfied smugness triggered the pain in her ribs again.

Astrid sneered at him. 'A group of archaeologists could

dig through your skull and still not find any evidence of intelligence, Colt. Why would I burn their faces with acid, and where did I get it? It was hardly inside my pockets when I went to that bar.'

Moore replied for him. 'Officers discovered a dozen containers of sulphuric acid in the Cruz garage.'

Of course they did.

'Where's Mr Cruz?' Astrid knew from experience that husbands or boyfriends were the main culprits in the deaths of wives, girlfriends and any family they had.

'Bob Cruz died five years ago. There was no significant other in Caitlin's life at the time of her death. We've checked all this, Ms Snow.'

She listened to Moore's words, considering what her next move could be.

'What about her work place? Plenty of murders are committed by disgruntled co-workers, and the use of the acid sounds like it was personal.'

'Caitlin Cruz worked in a church.'

Moore said that as if her employment meant everyone she worked with was exempt from committing a crime.

Chief Colt stood. 'That's enough for now; we ask the questions here, not you.' He nodded at Moore. 'You can continue this later once she's stewed long enough to think about her crimes.'

Moore turned to Astrid. 'Do you want to make your phone call?'

She deliberated on his question while images of Caitlin rattled through her head. Cruz had been kind to her, and they'd talked a little, though she couldn't remember what about, yet there were no memories of any children in that house when she was there.

But I didn't know a killer was there either.

Astrid decided against a lawyer, reluctantly admitting the only way out of this mess was back in England, but she didn't want to make the call to her former employers in the UK. There would be too many awkward silences and challenging questions: the silence from her, the probing from them. But she gave the number to Moore.

Let him sort it out.

'You need to ring these people. They'll straighten this out.'

He took the paper from her, and he and Colt left the room. The Officers dumped Astrid into the same cell, and she settled down and reached through her memories. She had a hyperactive deficiency disorder which messed up her brain if she didn't keep her thoughts moving. In times like this, since it wasn't her first incarceration, she grabbed at anything interesting she could remember.

She lay on the bed and searched her mind for some music. She selected the second Joy Division album from her internal jukebox and imagined she was in Manchester.

MOORE RETURNED LATER. Astrid had just finished some cardboard masquerading as meat and fruit juice squeezed from a dead donkey's balls. He pulled a chair closer to the bars. The look on his face told her it wasn't good news.

'Nobody is picking up on the other end of the number you gave me. Maybe I'll try again later, but I've got more questions first.'

Why not? She wasn't going anywhere in a hurry.

'Fire away, Detective.'

He took out a notebook. 'You strangled Caitlin Cruz

with a cloth from the kitchen, then stamped on her until you smashed her rib cage and chest. Then you poured acid onto her face, so there's nothing left to see.' He tapped his pen on the page. The noise irritated Astrid's ears.

'That sounds like a crime of passion.'

'You were angry because Starr beat you up with all those people watching. Then you lashed out at Cruz even though she helped you.'

'I was drunk, but I wasn't angry. And I didn't kill anyone.' This was a lot more personal than any anger she might have had. 'What happened with the children?'

Moore removed two pictures from his book and handed them to her. They weren't the images he'd shown her earlier, those innocent school photos of kids who'd never get the chance to grow up; these were carnage made real by an unhinged mind. Looking at dead bodies was nothing new to her, but this was different. Underneath the unrecognisable mess were humans whose faces had been burnt from their flesh, like their mother's. She flinched at the sight, thinking about the niece she hadn't spoken to in months. Then came the flash of memory, of the fight with the woman from the band. What else happened in Cruz's house? She couldn't remember, but something must have.

She rubbed at the top of her shoulder before handing the pictures back to Moore.

'What's the time of death for the kids compared to the mother?'

He scrutinised her. She wondered if he'd stopped giving her information. He was trying to manipulate her. That was obvious, but why if they had evidence and witnesses?

Of course, they don't have evidence and witnesses. I killed no one. Some thugs at the bar might have seen me getting into Cruz's car, but that meant nothing beyond she was helping me. And any decent defence attorney would rip the passport theory apart in seconds.

'The medical examiner reckons they died about thirty minutes after her.'

Astrid gripped on to the bars of the cell. 'You think they stood and watched while someone murdered their mother?'

'They might have seen you attack her. Is that why you killed them, to get rid of the witnesses?'

'Since we're having such a pleasant conversation, Detective, why don't you imagine for a second that I didn't kill any of them and consider all the other options?'

Moore rolled the pen between his fingers. 'Perhaps the kids were upstairs or out back and didn't know what was happening.'

'Were they deaf?' Astrid said.

'What?'

'Did those children have problems with their hearing?'

He looked through his notes. 'I don't think so.'

'Then why didn't they hear the attack on their mother? Caitlin would have made a lot of noise when someone covered her face in acid.' It was all in Astrid's head now, the violence and the sounds outside the bar and Cruz taking her home. Had her kindness got her and her children slaughtered in such a terrible fashion? 'I'm guessing the place was remote enough to have no neighbours, but those kids must've heard something.'

'That's not the only thing we can't explain.'

Astrid sat on the bed, letting the words hang in the air. He either expected her to break down and confess, or he needed help.

'You found something on the bodies.' She knew that made her sound like the killer.

'What did we find?' Moore got up.

She stared at the ceiling, her mind racing through crime scenes similar to the one they were accusing her of.

'Someone could have placed my passport there after they knocked me out. My fingerprints were in the house because I was there, and I bet you won't discover them on any of the bodies. Or anywhere apart from the kitchen. And certainly not upstairs, if that's where you found the kids.'

'What did we find?' Moore repeated.

She felt his breath through the bars and smelt the burnt wood of his aftershave. He wasn't wearing that earlier. Astrid swung around and faced the other wall.

'Somebody might have been there, waiting for me to leave before they struck. Perhaps they followed me to the bar as well. So there was more than one of them, and they lifted my passport from me when I passed out.' This wasn't random; the killer or killers had planned the murders. Then she'd come along and they'd used the opportunity, with the fight and her blacking out, to frame her. She looked at him.

'I don't know, Moore; what did you find?'

He stared at her. She knew the Detective shouldn't be speaking like this, understood he shouldn't be sharing information with her. But the murders had stumped him; she saw it in his eyes. He was intelligent, professional, intuitive. What was he doing in a small town like this?

Moore peered right through her. 'There was paper in each of their mouths.'

She didn't ask what was on the paper, though guessed there must have been something to have him so rattled. 'Maybe the frenzied attacks on the bodies weren't overkill, but something else?'

'Like what?'

'Perhaps it was to cover something up. Were those kids' arms covered in bruises?'

Moore stared at the photos again. 'Violence was all over them.'

'The excessive beating was a countermeasure, to hide the marks where somebody held them and forced them to watch while someone murdered their mother.'

Or maybe whoever did it enjoyed themselves too much.

'There was someone else there?' He didn't sound convinced.

'I'd guess at least two more people. The passport left behind is far too sloppy. Why would I be that sloppy?'

'I don't know.' His gaze pierced her. 'You were drunk, out of control; perhaps you didn't realise what you were doing.'

She went to the bed, lay down and stared at the ceiling.

'I think you better make that phone call again.'

Moore left Astrid on her own until an Officer brought her a sandwich and some coffee. It was the woman with the beautiful afro hair who'd taken her fingerprints earlier.

'Do you have any tea?'

'What?' The Officer opened her mouth wide enough for Astrid to glimpse her perfect teeth. What was it with Americans and the need to whiten everything? The confusion on her face made her even prettier.

'Can I have tea instead of coffee?' Astrid flashed her widest smile. 'It's a little reminder of home.'

'Sure,' she said and went and fetched it. After Astrid had drunk it, the same woman took her from the cell; there were no handcuffs this time. She peered at the Officer's badge as she left, not wanting to linger on her chest for too long.

'Thanks for that, Officer Campbell.' Campbell gave her a nod and led Astrid over to a chair at a large desk.

'Jim will be over in a second.'

'Jim?'

'Detective Moore.'

He stood in the far corner of the room, speaking to the Chief and some bloke Astrid didn't know. Even though they were inside, he wore sunglasses, like some rockstar trying to hang onto his fame. They finished talking, and turned to look at her. She sensed sympathy behind Moore's gaze, but the other two glared at her like frogs waiting to devour a fly. Moore strode towards her and sat on his side of the desk. She stared at it, noticing the lack of anything personal there, the void of family photos of any kind.

'Did you tell them it was likely at least three people killed Cruz and her kids?'

He avoided her gaze. 'I said it was a possibility.'

'You told them it was your idea, not mine?' He didn't reply. 'Did you make the phone call?'

'Not yet. If it was three killers, the Chief still thinks you were involved. Don't forget your prints were inside the house.'

'I told you what happened there.'

Moore placed his hands on the desk. 'It seems a lot of trouble to go to, to frame an outsider for three murders.'

'Killers will do anything to cover up their crimes; you should know that, Moore. I was unlucky enough to be the Oswald in the wrong place at the right time.'

He laughed at her. 'You don't think Oswald did it?'

'Not on his own.' She didn't know why Lee Harvey Oswald's name had sprung into her head at that precise moment, but it had.

Silence sat between them like a heavy stone.

'We need to lock you up again until I can make that call.' Moore didn't sound happy about it.

She accepted the inevitable, convinced it would be over

once they got the Agency on the other end of the phone. The Special Relationship between the British and American governments would help her for once.

'That's okay. That cell you had me in isn't too uncomfortable, and if you can get Officer Campbell to keep bringing me food, I'm sure the time will fly by.'

He nodded at her as the phone on the desk rang. Moore picked it up and placed it into the side of his head like a mould. He said nothing apart from the occasional yes with a nod, as if whoever was on the other end could see him.

'I understand,' he said before putting the phone down. His expression was one of deep unhappiness.

'Did you speak to my former employers?' Astrid said.

'No. I spoke to mine in Washington. They confirmed who you are after speaking to your former employers.' He glanced down at a note he'd made during the call. 'It's not MI5 or MI6, but something called the Agency?'

She ignored his question. 'You worked for the US Government?' The information surprised her.

'I still do,' he said, pulling at the badge on his jacket.

Astrid stood. 'Am I free to go?'

Moore's shoulders shrank into his chest. He pushed the passport towards her.

'We have witnesses putting you with Cruz not long before her murder; we have your fingerprints in the house, and we have that.' He pointed towards the bloody passport. 'Yet my instructions are to give it to you and let you go.' He didn't seem happy about it. 'I think certain people want you out of the country.'

Astrid picked it up, her fingers brushing against the small amount of dried blood clinging to the front.

'I've told you everything that happened, Detective. I'm

innocent, and you know it.' She slipped the passport into her pocket. 'Can I have my phone back?'

'We don't have that, Ms Snow.' She turned away from him. 'Don't you want to find out who framed you?'

'That's your job.' Astrid strode towards the door.

'Two kids died,' he shouted as she left the building. She stepped outside, unsure where she was and how to get back to that dump of a hotel and her stuff. The quicker she got out of town and on the road to Rochester, the better. If the Agency had used their influence to get her out of this mess, they'd expect something in return.

She was considering turning back into the police station to ask one of them which direction her hotel was in until the growl in her guts told her she needed food. That's when she remembered the map in the cell and how close Tom's Diner was.

Astrid's stomach led her from the cop shop and down the street to the diner. She was contemplating what American delicacies she'd have when the screaming came towards her.

4 PROBLEM CHILD

Two giant tumbleweeds rolled towards Astrid, kicking dirt and dust into the air. Only as she got closer to them did she realise it was teenagers fighting in the street. The noise they made was like a jet taking off. She didn't intervene in the conflict, joining the few others on the sidewalk in watching the early afternoon attraction. Punches were thrown and scratches bit into cheeks as memories of her teenage battles flashed through her head.

There were a few scraps during her adolescent years, both with boys and girls, but there was never something like this exhibition from a cartoon. Her favourite was a full-on battle in the school canteen with an older girl. She couldn't remember how it started, but would never forget how they fought over tables, scattering teachers and kids to the four corners, as they were covered in plates of beans and potatoes before an adult pulled them apart. The thought of it still had the power to resurrect the kitchen aromas in her nose.

As she relived more victories than defeats, the teenagers split apart like the atom and rolled in opposite directions.

The smaller one with dirty blonde hair arrived at Astrid's feet and scowled at her. The other one jumped up, the braces on her teeth glittering in the sun. For a frozen moment, the two antagonists glared at each other, and Astrid wondered if they were preparing to go again.

The one with the braces put an end to that thought.

'I'll see you later, Angie. There'll be nobody to protect you then.' She spat blood onto the ground and marched away, whistling some Taylor Swift tune Astrid knew Olivia liked. The constant image of her niece lingered in her head as she offered a hand to help Angie up. The grumpy girl refused and dusted herself down as she staggered to her feet. Astrid noted the cut on her nose and the clump of hair missing above her ear, thinking she made a good impersonation of a scarecrow at that moment.

Angie's eyes smouldered through a chilled expression.

'I don't need anyone's protection.'

There was something in the girl's defiance which reminded Astrid of her teenage self. 'I don't doubt it, Angie.'

The kid scrutinised her like a bug under a microscope. 'Do I know you, lady?'

Astrid shook her head. 'I'm just a stranger passing through town.'

Only she'd constipated the place and was now stuck somewhere in the bowels of Bakerstown. Angie laughed as she removed a bit of twig from her teeth.

'Good luck with that. Sometimes strangers don't get the warmest welcome here.'

The kid looked as if she hadn't eaten in days, with clothes which appeared like hand-me-downs from someone a few years older than her hanging off her bony frame. She flexed her fingers and shook the dirt from her shoulders. Her gaze buried deep into Astrid as she took one step back.

The rest of the onlookers had returned to their business and there was only them in the street.

'Why don't you tell me what to avoid while I'm here, and I'll buy you a meal?' Astrid nodded towards the diner. 'I'm heading there now.'

Angie's eyes narrowed into pinpricks. 'Are you a psycho out to rape and kill me?'

Astrid's ribs ached as she tried to contain her laughter.

'How am I going to do that in a diner full of people?'

The girl ran a hand through her tangled hair and stepped closer to Astrid.

'Where are you from?'

'England.'

'Is that why you have a funny accent?'

'I guess so.'

'I hope you have plenty of money as well.'

She turned on her heels and marched towards the diner. Astrid followed and wondered what she'd let herself in for.

The floor in Tom's Diner was a spotless checkerboard pattern, its layout combining narrow red-hued booths, silver enamel bar stools, and circular tables. The lunchtime crowd was in full swing as the two of them moved inside, the noise dropping a little as customers and staff glanced at the newcomers. Astrid guessed they were looking at her more than the girl. When she peered into the eyes of those who didn't flinch from her gaze, she saw curiosity in their faces, which probably came from her reputation as a potential murderer.

Before anyone asked questions and scared the kid away, Astrid led her into the nearest booth. She grabbed the menu as her legs squeaked against the bright red leather. She didn't need to go through the choices since her brain and stomach could already smell the aroma of barbecue chicken wings drafting from the kitchen.

As her guts grumbled again, Angie grabbed the menu from her.

'Your stomach sounds like how I feel.'

Astrid checked she still had money in her pockets. It was at that point she wondered where her phone had gone. She searched through her jacket and trousers more than once before admitting her mobile had gone the same way as her passport. The thought of the killer or killers who'd murdered the Cruz family having her phone made her temple throb.

As she dug through the dark spots of her memory again, the server came to take their order. Angie went about getting one of nearly everything on the menu. Astrid grinned at her.

'You weren't wrong about me needing plenty of money, were you?'

'Never turn down free food, even if it's from some weirdo English woman.'

Astrid removed her jacket as the server returned with her coffee and Angie's colossal glass of Coke and a long pink straw. Angie slurped half the drink as she spoke.

'So what do you want from me?'

Astrid fiddled with the salt and pepper set on the table. 'Why would I want something from you?'

The kid nearly snorted Coke all over herself. 'Give me a break, lady. No oldie does something like this with someone like me for nothing. If you were a guy, I'd say you're a creeper or predator, not that women can't be those, but I think you're after something else.'

'Such as?'

The server brought over a large order of fries, which Angie covered in ketchup.

'I guess you'll tell me at some point.'

Astrid felt every eye in the diner on her and decided there was no need to mess around.

'Did you know Caitlin Cruz?'

Red sauce dripped from Angie's lips. 'The woman murdered last night?' She supped at the Coke and pushed her back into the booth. Astrid assumed the girl must have had a sudden revelation. 'You're the one they arrested for killing her.'

There was no point lying to her. 'I am.'

Does everyone know that?

From the way it felt as if the gaze of the world was upon her, she supposed they did.

'That's why all the mugs in here are staring at you. Not 'cause you're a stranger, but 'cause you're a killer.'

She couldn't deny that charge. 'I didn't kill Cruz or her kids.'

This time, the kid did spit Coke over her legs. 'Someone murdered Cathy and Dale as well?'

The shock on her face sent a stab of pain through Astrid's damaged ribs.

'Did you know them?'

Angie bit through bun and burger, dripping melted cheese and onions on to her fingers. She licked the detritus from her flesh as someone put Bruce Springsteen on the jukebox.

'I went to school with Cathy, same year and some of the same classes. Dale is, was, five years younger than her. Damn!' She grimaced in the way kids do when masking their nervousness.

'Did you know Cathy's mother?'

The server brought the rest of their order over as Astrid waited for an answer. Angie finished the fries and returned to her burger, crunching through soggy looking salad as she spoke.

'I used to see her at school when Cathy and I were younger, but not for a long time. I think she was too busy working at her church.'

Astrid remembered the map in her cell, picturing the two churches on opposite sides of Main Street. They were probably a fifteen-minute walk from where she sat.

'She worked for a church, or she ran her own?'

Angie shrugged. 'No idea. She wasn't one of those fundamentalists or anything. I know that for a fact.'

The kid had relaxed and loosened up, perhaps helped by the amount of food she'd consumed in a short space of time.

'How do you know that?'

'Because she let Cathy behave like a normal teenager. There was none of that "You can't do this" or "You can't do that because the bible says so" nonsense.'

'Did you know Cathy well?'

'We hung out in the same places and liked the same things. And I saw her at school before I stopped going.'

'Why don't you go to school?'

Angie sucked Coke through the straw. 'None of your business, lady.' She burped loudly enough to attract the attention of the other diners. 'What's your name, anyway?'

'I'm Astrid.'

'So, Astrid, you didn't kill the Cruzes?'

'No. Was Caitlin Cruz with someone?'

The Coke glugged down Angie's throat. 'I dunno. Cathy mentioned no one to me.'

'No father on the scene?' Astrid remembered Moore or

Colt telling her that Mr Cruz had died, but she wanted to see if Angie knew that.

The girl shrugged. 'Some dads of Bakerstown don't hang around for long once the mothers' spit out their brats.'

'Did yours?'

'None of your business.'

'Where's your mother?'

'At work.'

'Why don't you go to school?'

'None of your BIZZ NESS.'

Her tone rattled the light fittings above them. The kid had demolished a family meal while Astrid had barely touched hers. She leant closer to Angie so none of the ear grabbers in the diner would hear what she said.

'Can you think of anyone who would want to harm them?'

Angie burped again and raised her voice, uncaring if anyone heard her or not.

'Everyone has secrets, Astrid.' She wiped Coke from her lips. 'I bet you've got a few.'

Astrid studied the teenage girl's face, examining every movement she made, including the slight twitch in her eyebrows and how her bottom lip trembled. She was hiding something, but what?

'Do you know what *quid pro quo* means, Angie?'

The kid shook her head and laughed. 'I might not go to school, but I'm not stupid, Astrid. You want something from me, and you'll give me something in return. I knew you were after something, and I told you that.' She moved the plate to the side. 'You fed me up like poor old Hansel and Gretel.'

'I'm only after information, nothing else.'

'That's why I'm answering your questions, aren't I?'

'Do you have a cell phone?'

'Of course.'

Astrid removed money from her pocket and pushed it across the table towards Angie.

'Can you get me one and keep it quiet? I lost mine last night.'

Angie scooped up the cash without counting it.

'No problem, Astrid. You want it to be untraceable?'

'Can you do that?'

'That's easy peasy, English lady.'

'That's impressive for a fifteen-year-old.'

Angie stood. 'You ain't seen nothing yet, Astrid.'

'I'm staying at the Gillespie Inn. Do you know it?'

She laughed loudly enough to turn the heads who weren't already scrutinising them. 'That dump? I'm not going to your hotel room so you can murder me. No, I'll tell you when I've got what you want.'

Then she left with a flourish, banging the door behind her as she went. Astrid settled in to finish her food in peace, only it didn't last long.

'What were you doing talking to the Delaney girl?'

Inside her head, someone sang about using tears for shields and spears as she nibbled on a salty fry. She cricked her neck to twist her gaze towards the tall slabs of American beef hovering over her. She'd noticed them on the way in, wearing cowboy hats even though she guessed they were a long way from cowboy territory. One hat was brilliant white, the other obsidian black.

The one with the black hat spoke to her.

'You should leave the Delaney kid alone.'

Astrid assumed they meant Angie. 'How can I help you, gents?'

They planted their hands on the table and leant towards her.

'If you hurt any more of our people, lady, then you'll pay for it. Do you understand that?'

She pressed her fingers into her ribs, contemplating if she wanted to get into another conflict in the town. She'd only just escaped from a police cell, so engaging in another skirmish wasn't recommended.

Astrid pushed the remains of her food aside and stood, the top of her head brushing the arm of the closest of her new friends.

'I'll be sure to take your advice.'

She threw money on to the table and turned from them, the hairs on the back of her neck bristling from the stale heat of their breath. She marched out of Tom's Diner and into the afternoon sun, unsure of where her hotel was. It may have been a dump, but it still contained what little she had to her name.

'Do you want a lift?' Officer Campbell stood at her side.

'Is that allowed?' Astrid's smile consumed her.

'I've finished my shift, so I can do what I want.'

She found it difficult to contain her grin. 'Well, what's a woman to do on an afternoon in a one-horse town?'

'I'm sure we can find something,' Officer Campbell said as she led Astrid to her car.

———

SOMETIME LATER, Astrid slipped from the bed and admired the curve of Campbell's naked back.

'Is this what they call afternoon delight?'

The policewoman handed her a drink. 'Well, it's the afternoon, and it's delightful.'

Astrid sipped at her glass. 'It's a shame I'll be leaving tomorrow.'

The bourbon warmed her throat as she gazed around the apartment. It had been a short drive from the diner, and there'd been little talk between them during it. Even less once they got inside and she'd succumbed to Officer Campbell pulling her clothes off. There was little time to take in her surroundings then, so now she scanned Campbell's home environment.

In new places, residential places, she always judged people by what they owned; she classed their usefulness to her by what they read or listened to or watched. How interesting they were, beyond sex, was defined by what she perceived as their cultural baggage. So it was disappointing to see nothing in the apartment apart from a three-day-old local newspaper and a tattered copy of *Ready Player One*.

Campbell leant forward. 'Do you have to go?'

Astrid gazed at her. It was tempting; she was very tempting. If it wasn't for the burn mark on her cheek, she could have graced the cover of any glamour magazine. Astrid reached up to touch it, wondering if Campbell would stop her, glad when she didn't. The scar was smoother than she expected, and her fingers tingled with desire as she caressed the police Officer's face.

'I could stay for a few more days.'

But she needed to return to England and repair things with her sister. Not that she was keen to speak to Courtney, but she missed her niece so much. And then there was Rochester and a grave to visit. She wanted to put fresh flowers on it and remember something good from her childhood.'

There was hesitation in Campbell's voice, a shyness which wasn't there earlier.

'Or you could stay around and help those idiots I work with solve this case. Nobody can figure out what those numbers are for.'

Astrid finished her drink and returned to the bed, her skin aching at the warmth of the other woman's body.

'What numbers?'

Campbell kissed her on the forehead, and then the bridge of her nose.

'I shouldn't tell you this, but I'm talking about the numbers on those bits of paper found inside the victims' mouths. Four on one, four on another, and two on the last one. Forensics has gone through any combination of phone numbers, but come up with nothing so far.'

Astrid stared at the paperback book sitting all alone on the shelf. 'Do you have a Cybercrime unit at the station?'

Campbell laughed and grabbed Astrid's hand. 'Including me, there's about eight of us down there, half of whom can't even use a cell phone, never mind a computer. Why?'

Astrid rolled out of bed and reached for her trousers. 'Do you want me to stay?' Campbell nodded. 'Then you need to take me back to the idiots at the station.'

5 SANCTUM SANCTORUM

They got dressed and left. Officer Campbell moved to the car before Astrid stopped her.

'Has Moore spoken to anyone at Cruz's workplace?'

'Not that I'm aware of, but he wouldn't be keeping me informed, anyway.'

'Do you know which church Caitlin worked at?'

Campbell took out her phone. 'I don't, but I can soon find out.'

Two minutes later, they drove along Main Street to the First Church of the Baptist. They parked next to a sign proclaiming the Home of the Bakerstown Bears. They got out of the car, and Astrid stared at the grain silos and wind turbines connecting the hills to the clouds. The church was a modern building, all red brick and white trim, standing alone with fields on either side. The roof sloped from right to left, and underneath was a large cross positioned so that, when the sunlight hit it just right, like it was then, its shadow stretched over the rest of the church and out into the street. The tip of it reached Astrid's shoes as she glanced behind her towards the much less imposing and far more weather-beaten United Methodist Church.

'I guess we know where most of the religious donations in the town go, Officer Campbell, but isn't there conflict from the different congregations with the two churches being so close?'

She shook her head. 'Conflicts of any kind are few in Bakerstown. A little over five thousand people live here, and most of us get along fine, even if there are a few differences of opinion on religion or politics.'

Astrid hadn't noticed any political sloganeering for any party during her stay, but then this was the only time she'd seen the place during the day. She stared at Campbell's police uniform and wished they were back at the Officer's apartment, yet it still didn't cross her mind to ask for the other woman's first name.

'Are you religious, Officer Campbell?'

'I have plenty of faith, Snow, but you'll have to get to know me better to find out what in.'

Astrid grinned as they strode up the steps.

'Do we knock or go straight in?'

Before Campbell could reply, the large entrance opened and a tall, imposing man greeted them.

'Welcome to the First Church of the Baptist, ladies. We are all children under God. I'm Joe Rennie, the Minister here. How can I help you?'

Some people flash a smile when they greet you, but this bloke was the smile. Joy radiated out of every inch of him. Astrid thought the tequila and the beating were playing tricks on her until she realised the light shimmering around his frame was only the sun reflecting off the whitewashed wall behind him. He looked like a marine, and Astrid imagined him leading troops into battle.

Campbell thrust her hand towards him. 'We've met before, Minister Rennie, at the police charity drive for the destitute and the homeless.' He took her grasp. 'I'm Officer Campbell, and this is Special Agent Astrid Snow with British Intelligence. Can we speak to you inside?'

Rennie's eyes bulged with surprise, but Astrid guessed he was no more shocked by Campbell's words than she was.

'My, my; British Intelligence, you say.' He scrutinised her like an astronomer thinking they'd discovered life on Mars. 'That sounds very glamorous indeed. What can we do for you?'

Campbell placed one hand on her hip. 'It would be better if we could speak inside.'

He appeared to consider her request for a second.

'Of course, ladies, please come in, but mind the mess.'

Astrid flashed Campbell a look of *What The Fuck?* as they followed him into the church. The space was long and wide, with two sets of chairs in rows down either side. There were groups of fresh flowers alongside the seats, filling the air with a mixed aroma of roses and gardenias. At the bottom was what she assumed was the stage for the sermons.

She glanced over the seats and what filled them.

'Are you collecting for something, Minister?'

Most of the chairs contained bags full of clothes and shoes. Below them stood boxes of food and bottles of water.

Rennie's grin continued to glow.

'We provide these things for whoever needs them. In difficult economic times, we must all do what we can for those less fortunate than us, and the church should play a leading role in that.' His smile wavered a little, but the sparkle grew behind his eyes as he studied her. 'You appear to be a long way from home, Agent Snow. How can the First Church of the Baptist help you?'

She decided not to tell him she was plain old Astrid Snow, thinking the misconception Campbell had created might aid her.

'We're here about one of your employees, Caitlin Cruz.'

'We're an equal congregation, Agent Snow. There is no hierarchy of bishops or priests exercising authority over members. The church is self-governing and self-supporting, made up of members, each with a role to play. We encourage those attending to become members through baptism, which entitles them to vote at the church meeting where all decisions occur. Final authority rests not with the Minister or Deacons, but with church members.'

It was a nice little speech, and she wondered if he was aware of Cruz's murder and the long spiel was a delaying tactic. If Angie Delaney knew about Caitlin's death, and it seemed the rest of those in the diner knew of the murders, too, then surely he did?

Campbell stepped forward to do her duties. 'We have some bad news about Caitlin, Minister Rennie.'

The light disappeared from him. 'Yes, Officer Campbell, I'm aware of what happened to Caitlin and her children.' He twisted his head to gaze at the large painting of Jesus on the ceiling. 'They are all with Our Lord now, in a much better place than this world.'

Astrid gave him the benefit of the doubt and assumed he was containing his grief because he truly believed they were better off.

'Can you tell us what work she did for the church?'

He lowered his head to stare at her, providing an expression she wasn't unfamiliar with: that look certain people had when they believed they were not only the most important person in the room, but probably the world as well. She'd seen it from presidents and prime ministers, kings and queens, CEOs and managers, generals and majors, crime lords and drug barons, and even from serial killers, but this was the first time from a man of God.

'Nobody should be defined by their work, Agent Snow.' The way he emphasised her name, she wished she'd put him straight about her lowly position in the world. 'We are a church of ordinary and imperfect humans who seek to live their lives by following Jesus and the way he lived. We've found he has welcomed us "home" with open arms and transformed our lives, and so we aim to be an informal, welcoming church that helps others follow Jesus, too. We desire to be a place where people, regardless of age, gender, background and ethnicity, can belong and find a sense of purpose. Everybody in the church contributes the same, irrespective of their work.'

She wondered if she'd somehow offended him and if he'd got the wrong impression of what she was looking for from the question.

Campbell spoke up before Astrid could.

'We need to get an idea of Caitlin's life outside of her family, Minister Rennie, so we can create a profile of her, to see who she might have come into contact with who would do such a terrible thing to her and the children.'

He placed one hand on the back of the nearest chair. 'You believe her time here may have led Caitlin's killer to her?'

He gazed straight through Astrid as he spoke. She said nothing, letting her new partner reply.

'Anything we learn about her activities with the church might help in the investigation.'

The shadow of darkness that had crept over his face for

the last two minutes disappeared with the return of his broad smile.

'Please, ladies, call me Joe.' He moved to the side and pointed towards the pulpit. 'If you follow me, I'll give you a tour while I explain Caitlin's time here.'

He led them between the chairs, and then turned right before they reached the dais, taking them through a door and into another large room. There was a faint smell of chlorine in the air, and it didn't surprise Astrid to see most of the space taken up by a small swimming pool.

'Do you perform many baptisms, Joe?'

The glint in his eyes sparkled even more brightly with her question. 'It depends on the time of year.' He opened out his broad shoulders and pointed towards the water. 'This is our baptistery. Caitlin and others helped me with the baptisms.'

'Were there any duties or responsibilities Caitlin undertook more than others?'

They'd reached the pool, and he rested his arm on the podium. She glanced at his reflection rippling in the water, watching it twist and shiver to resemble something not quite human.

'Even within the church, Caitlin differed from most.' He peered towards the far window which looked upon the town. 'At the end of a long day, many of us turn to the box or the internet to relax, but she had no interest in those things. When she wasn't helping others, she liked nothing better than putting her head between a book's pages. She never watched television or movies, spending most of her free time reading. Caitlin believed TV was for lazy people, whereas reading made the brain work hard to fit in all the bits the writer had left out. She was also a great believer in the written word helping those who struggle to string sentences together as they get older.'

Astrid had wondered where he was going with this information, but now she knew.

'She went into the community to help those with dementia or Alzheimer's, taking books to them and getting them to read?'

He nodded. 'Caitlin did all that and more, Agent Snow. She had great success with it, visited many homes in town, and improved people's lives. Her death is a terrible loss for all of us, and the same for her children. Cathy and Dale had many friends who will miss them.'

Campbell stepped closer to him. 'Did you ever see anyone suspicious-looking hanging around the church?'

Rennie furrowed his eyebrows. 'What do you mean by suspicious-looking?' He peered at Astrid. 'Are you talking about foreigners?'

The policewoman shook her head. 'Anybody who might have seemed out of place or up to no good.'

'I can't say I did.' He reached down into a podium door and removed a sash which he placed around his neck. 'Do you think Caitlin met her killer in the church? I find that hard to believe.'

A group of people entered the room, marching around the pool's far side and taking seats opposite Astrid and Campbell. It was a mixture of men and women of varying ages, but she recognised one of them: the diner's white-hatted cowboy. He tilted his hat at her as she refocused on the Minister.

Astrid didn't pull any punches. 'Bad people are found in every walk of society, Joe; even churches.'

He glanced across at his flock. 'I know that only too

well, Agent Snow. I moved to Bakerstown twenty years ago after leaving the place of my birth, believing everywhere on this planet was nothing but a sewer of sin and deceit. I left convinced that towns like my own were cesspits of intolerance and meanness, hiding behind a disguise of folksiness. Fortunately, I found the Lord during my travels, and now I understand there's a positive reaction to counter every sinful action. And Caitlin performed enough positive actions to balance out the negative in this town for a long time.'

She didn't have the heart to question his belief and ask him how the murder of an innocent woman and two children could ever find a counterweight in this world. So she asked him something else instead.

'Do you have a list of those Caitlin visited when working in the community?'

She expected him to refuse and was surprised when he didn't.

'If you tell me your cell number, I'll text the file to you.'

'I lost my phone last night.' She glanced at her partner. 'Officer Campbell will give you hers.'

Which she did. 'You store church data on your cell, Joe?'

He took a phone from his pocket. 'Caitlin was the one who convinced me we should keep a record of all our activities, and there should be digital copies stored securely online on my cell and the church's computer network.' Astrid was admiring the efficiency of it when Campbell's phone pinged with an incoming message. 'Now, if you don't mind, I have today's baptisms to complete.'

He left them to go to the group waiting by the pool as Campbell stared at the file on her cell.

'Is there anything useful in what he sent?' Astrid said.

Campbell handed her the phone. 'There are a dozen

names here, most of which I recognise, but nothing jumps out at me as suspicious.'

Astrid read through them and thought the same until she came to the last one. She returned the phone to Campbell. 'Do you know the woman at the end of the list?'

Campbell stared at it. 'I do; we were at school together. Why?'

Astrid watched as Minister Joe Rennie went about his work, climbing into the pool and beckoning the first of his flock to follow him.

'Because I think I might have had lunch with Maggie Delaney's daughter a few hours ago.' She returned Campbell's phone to her.

'Angie? You were in the diner with Angie Delaney?' Astrid nodded. Campbell's eyes narrowed. 'Why?'

'She was fighting in the street with another girl when I left the police station. When they stopped tearing seven bells out of each other, the kid looked so malnourished, I thought she needed a decent meal.'

Campbell sucked in her lips and eyed Astrid suspiciously. 'Really?'

'Why not? I'm a stranger in town, and kids are always helpful to strangers.'

'Are you kidding me?'

'Nope. Why would I do that?'

'Okay, I'll believe you for now. But what has you eating with Angie Delaney and her mother's name being on this list got to do with the Cruz murders?'

'I don't know, maybe nothing. I just think it's curious. Angie said she wasn't going to school, but wouldn't tell me why when I asked. Perhaps it's because she's staying home as her mother has dementia.'

She watched the exasperation move across Campbell's face.

'I don't understand what that's got to do with trying to find who killed Caitlin Cruz and her children.'

'Let's just call it a hunch.' Astrid flashed her partner the widest of grins. 'Do you know where the Delaneys live?'

Campbell's eyebrows reached for the sky as her lips stretched wide. 'You want to visit them now?'

Astrid shook her head. 'We'll talk to Moore about some numbers first.'

6 ALONE AGAIN OR

'We should tell Detective Moore about your hunch.'

They'd stopped for gas on the way to the police station. Astrid disagreed with Campbell's suggestion as they got out of the car.

'No, let's wait for now. These numbers they found are more important to focus on.'

She stretched her legs while Campbell bought cigarettes. Astrid pushed her shoulders back and breathed in everything around her, not just the air, but the whole experience of America. She'd dreamed of this since she was a small girl, watching the flickering lights of the television while locked inside her room for twelve hours a day. This was her *High Sierra*, her *Key Largo*, and her *Kiss Me Deadly*.

That's what she'd told herself when she'd first arrived in the town.

She'd been in Bakerstown less than an hour when she went to the bar after dumping what little she had in the cheapest hotel she could find. It was dark when she got there, and she'd got drunk a lot quicker than expected, which might have had something to do with the fact she hadn't eaten for twenty-four hours.

The beers and tequila which followed didn't help her state of mind that night, but only exacerbated the grumpiness flowing through her; a gnawing irritant she knew came from her sister's refusal to answer any of her phone calls, texts, or emails. Not that she even wanted to speak to Courtney; it was her niece's voice she needed to hear. Olivia was ever present in her thoughts and the lack of contact with her drove Astrid's misery to greater lengths by the day.

At least she was doing something she'd dreamed of since she was a kid: to travel across America and see some of its sights. Now, she saw Bakerstown in the daylight and took it all in. A vast swathe of rolling hills stood in the distance on the other side of the gas station; brilliant shades of red and green rose into the sky as a flock of birds sauntered overhead.

She peered into the sun and remembered her favourite Tears For Fears video as a car as big as a truck pulled up next to them. A woman climbed out of it as if she was preparing for the catwalk, wearing impossibly high heels and a dress painted on to her bones. The hair on her head must have had enough spray on it to decimate the ozone layer. A man got out the other side, as tall as a giraffe with shoulders borrowed from a bull. His hat was bigger than his head.

Campbell gave them a respectful nod as she left the shop, and the couple entered.

'Friends of yours?' Astrid said as they returned to the car.

'Hardly,' Campbell replied. 'That's Jimmy and Rosie

Sawyer, twins and only kids to old man Sawyer. They'll own this town once he's gone.'

'Their father owns everything here?'

'He does; all that's worth owning and a little that isn't.'

'Does that include some residents?'

Campbell didn't answer the question, but threw Astrid one of her own. 'There's a rumour going around you came here to find a grave. Is that true?'

Astrid placed a hand above her head to keep the sun from her eyes as it shone through the windscreen. A small dog strolled in front of them, cocked its skinny leg, and pissed over the car. The stink of urine seeped through the open windows as the policewoman shouted at the mutt; it scampered away as she yelled at it.

Astrid snatched the can of Coke Campbell offered her, opened it, and drank half in one go. The cold bubbles tickled the back of her throat and distracted her from the ache in her ribs.

'As a kid, I was fascinated by old movies. The black and white ones from the silent era and the twenties and thirties, before the Hollywood censors arrived and ruined everything. They were an escape into a different world, a better one than my own. Chaplin, Keaton and the Marx Brothers made me laugh; Lugosi and Karloff scared me; *Metropolis* and *King Kong* sent me into new realms of adventure, while I fell in love with Harlow, Garbo and Valentino. But there was only one person who captured my heart.' She pressed the chilled can against her face, absorbing the dampness into her skin as a shield from the sun. 'I came to America by accident, but while I'm here, on an unexpectedly extended stay, I promised I'd see where that person is buried, in Rochester.'

Campbell didn't appear to be affected by the heat. 'That's cool. Are you going to tell me their name?'

Astrid finished the drink and dropped the can into the slot in the car door. 'While I'm here, I'll give you some clues to guess who it is. As long as you don't cheat and use the internet.'

Campbell shook her head. 'As if I don't have enough to think about.'

'You don't want to amuse me?'

'Go on, then, give me the first clue, but if you're talking about someone famous nearly a hundred years ago, they better be good clues if you want me to guess their name.'

'She left home at sixteen to become a dancer in New York City.'

Campbell's laughter bounced through the car. 'Brilliant. Thanks a lot, my English friend.'

Astrid ignored her partner's grumpiness and flicked the switch to the jukebox in her head to sing out loud to the music only she could hear as they left.

Campbell glanced at her. 'What's that tune?'

'*Sunday Morning* by the Velvet Underground. Is this a new one to you?'

'No, I know it; I just didn't recognise your mangled version of it.'

They laughed together as Campbell drove.

The drive there was quick. Bakerstown was a narrow maze of streets, everywhere free of litter, with the buildings a mix of the old and the new. It could have been a small town anywhere, but the one thing that caught Astrid's attention was the large brewery near the police station. The sight of the logo on its gates, of a bear sitting inside a beer glass, triggered the smell of alcohol in her nose.

And then she remembered the image from the bar and

the beers she'd drunk. The cartoon bear stared at her and clawed at the back of her skull, trying to retrieve her missing memories, but it was no good. She shook it from her head as Campbell parked and they stepped into the station.

No one inside appeared pleased to see them. Moore slammed the phone down and had a face like a bulldog chewing a wasp as Astrid approached his desk. His eyes narrowed when he spoke to her.

'Have you returned to help with the investigation into the murders of Caitlin Cruz and her children?'

'Can you show me the bits of paper you removed from the victims' mouths?' She expected he wouldn't, but asked anyway.

Moore opened a drawer. 'I'm not allowed to share anything with you, Snow, but I will place this photocopy of them on the desk before I hand it to Officer Campbell.'

He did that. She stared at the numbers and memorised them as Campbell grabbed the paper before anyone else noticed what was happening.

'What do you think they mean?'

He stared long and hard at her, and she guessed he was wondering how much he should tell her. After a minute of silence, he gave in.

'We figure it's a phone number with one digit missing, stuffed into their mouths because it's some psycho ritual or they're playing games with us.' Moore gazed right at her. 'Unless you know something we don't.'

She pulled up a chair to rest her aching feet. The afternoon exercise had taken more out of her than she'd thought possible. And her ribs were throbbing again.

'You're wrong on both counts, Detective.'

She waited for him to ask why, but it was Campbell who spoke first.

'Why do you say that, Astrid?'

She liked the way her name sounded on Campbell's lips, but she also noticed Moore's grimace.

'The paper wasn't stuffed into their mouths for some serial killer to get their kicks. I think the victims were trying to hide the numbers or swallow them.'

'Why would they do that?' Moore crossed his arms.

'I'm guessing they lead back to whoever killed them,' Astrid replied.

'But they're not part of a phone number?' Campbell said.

Astrid smiled at Moore. 'Can I borrow your computer?'

He got out of his chair. 'Be my guest.'

Astrid went to the other side of the desk while they watched what she was doing. She brought up the web browser and opened another tab away from the county police force's website. She cleared the address and typed in the numbers from memory. It came back as page not found. Then she switched the two groups of four around and retried again. She got the same results: page not found. She tried every combination, but ended up with dead pages each time.

She grabbed a pen from Moore's desk and used the end to poke at her palm.

Moore seemed perturbed by her action.

'What are you doing?'

'I was sure those numbers were a website address.'

Campbell put her fingers on to Astrid's hand and took the pen from her. 'I thought web addresses were all www this or www another.'

Astrid twisted her head to smile at her. 'No, that's just what the numbers are converted into to make it easier for the public to use. The URLs contain ten numbers.'

Moore raised his eyebrows at her. 'URLs?'

Astrid gazed at the screen. 'Universal Resource Locators.'

She crunched the front part of her brain until a memory returned of her father beating her one night after he'd found her diary and discovered what she'd written about him. The pain of the image was terrible, but it ignited a flashbulb in her head. She'd continued writing in her diary, but to stop him from reading it, she'd invented her own code. Not that complex, but enough to fool him.

Cyphers and maps had always fascinated her, to the point she'd started creating her own regularly; she'd used the codes to keep certain things secret from adults and her sister. The maps had been her way of coping with emotional problems; she'd used them as plans for her escape to a better life. Nowadays, she created maps in her head as a way of solving complex problems. This was now second nature to her, so much so she devised a new one using the figures she'd memorised until she hit on a solution.

She tried the numbers again, but this time in combinations of reverse order. She got the right one on the fourth attempt.

Moore and Campbell gasped at the sight. Astrid accepted it as inevitable when the website popped up. Someone selling people online like they were cheap shoes or dishcloths was nothing new to her.

Moore turned the screen towards him. 'It's a human trafficking site.'

Astrid wondered how long she had left in the town. She got up as Moore flicked through the pages, not envying him the sights he was about to see.

She looked at Campbell.

'You should contact your local FBI office to deal with this.'

I've done my part now. That website will link to Caitlin's killers.

Moore gritted his teeth, an audible sound which hurt her ears.

'But why would they kill Caitlin Cruz and her kids?'

Astrid shrugged. 'Ask the people behind the website when you find them.'

She was heading for the door as Moore's phone rang. Her hand was on the handle of the exit when he shouted to her.

'I need your help, Snow.' She didn't know whether to be flattered or worried, considering he'd said it in front of his colleagues. Most of them pretended not to notice, but she felt their eyes burrowing into her.

Astrid waited for the inevitable.

'There's been another murder.'

IT WAS TWO MURDERS, and it took them twenty-five minutes to get to the crime scene. She travelled with Moore, resisting the temptation of sitting next to Campbell in the other car. They spent most of the journey in silence. The Detective's gaze focused on the road while Astrid scruti-nised the surroundings.

Bakerstown looked like a sleepy, slightly eccentric country place where nothing much happened. Problems were mild and manageable, and conflicts solved through neighbourliness and the application of common sense.

But as idyllic as it seemed, she guessed there would be darkness in a town like this. Wherever you found people, you'd get sin and failing. Moore's faith in his fellow humans in Bakerstown was admirable, but she recognised it was misguided.

She studied his face as he drove, understanding that if anyone knew where this town's failings were located, it was likely to be him. His gaze peered through the glass in front of him, and she would have sworn he'd aged rapidly since their first meeting. Dark brown eyes filled with obvious pain and hidden trauma glistened in the light. But then, she didn't feel too good herself.

I should get him to drop me at the bus station. Nothing is keeping me here now.

But her memories of that night were incomplete, and if she couldn't resurrect them, they'd keep on haunting her, regardless of where she went.

Astrid broke the silence. 'Are you allowed to take me to a crime scene?'

'You're aiding with an investigation; that's all anyone needs to know.'

His New York accent told her he wasn't originally from the town. Now they were alone, his speech was slower than before, the words slipping from his mouth at a languid pace. They arrived and met Campbell. Astrid gazed at her, still surprised she didn't know her first name.

Don't kid yourself. You don't want to know because you're leaving here soon, and it's best not to get too attached.

She thought of this as she checked the area, wondering why there weren't more vehicles apart from theirs and one other police car. Then she remembered what Campbell had told her about the limited police resources.

Now all three of them and the one-horse town's only forensic guy stood inside a cabin on the outskirts. Only the forensic guy was a woman, and Astrid was happy about that for more than one reason. Her name was Alice Graves, which seemed highly appropriate to Astrid.

Graves sounded tired when she spoke.

'We've got a male and female bludgeoned to death about eight hours ago with a yet undiscovered weapon.' She glanced at Astrid, but didn't ask what the stranger was doing there.

Astrid knelt to look closer. Moore had given her some forensic gloves, but she had no desire to touch anything. The two bodies lay close together, hands outstretched to reach each other, but failing by a few inches. The killer had smashed their fingers into blood and pulp, a destruction that matched what was left of both their heads, which appeared to have taken a bath in a heavy dose of sulfuric acid. The smell of burnt flesh lingered in the air.

Campbell stood next to Astrid. 'It looks like someone tried to cover up their identities.'

Astrid turned to Moore. 'Do you know who lived here?'

He got out his cell and dialled a number which she assumed was the police station. She was still annoyed she didn't have her phone.

He was on his cell for two minutes. In that time, she scanned the cabin and the immediate exterior. The place stood on its own, with no other residences in sight. Trees surrounded it, and she guessed its owners used it for tourists and holidaymakers.

When she returned inside, he'd finished the call and confirmed her thoughts.

'This is a holiday home and nobody has rented it for six months.'

'Who owns it?' She stared at the bodies again, her eyes fixed on those hands, reaching out to each other but not getting there.

Moore put his phone away. 'No need to check for that information. That would be Benedict Sawyer.'

'Old man Sawyer?' Astrid said.

'You know him?' Moore replied.

'We saw the twins earlier,' Campbell added.

Astrid turned to Alice Graves. 'This is the work of the same killer or killers from the Cruz murders?'

Her skin was soft and pale, with a layer of freckles under both eyes. Those eyes sparkled with intelligence as Graves brushed a stray wisp of hair behind her ear, touching her high cheekbones as she did. Her lips glistened as she spoke.

'Either that or it's a very skilled copycat.'

Astrid stared at what remained of the victims' faces. 'Did you find anything unusual in their mouths?'

'Only smashed teeth and blood.'

Campbell and Moore checked the cabin. Astrid addressed the Detective when they'd finished.

'Have you found any clues?'

He shook his head. 'Not yet.'

She took one last look at the bloodied things that used to be people on the floor.

'Then we must wait until you hear from the FBI about that website.'

'We?' Moore looked at her curiously.

'Unless you want me to leave?'

The Detective scowled. 'No, Ms Snow; I think I'll need all the help I can get.'

She couldn't tell if that was sarcasm or not. Astrid turned to Campbell.

'Then the only thing to work out is where I'm going to stay, because I can't stomach another night in that hotel. What do you say, Officer Campbell?'

I don't even know her first name.

Moore slapped Astrid on the back. 'I doubt Campbell's husband will take kindly to having a limey Brit in the house with them; he's not a big fan of foreigners, is he, Eleanor?'

Astrid stared at Officer Eleanor Campbell, watching the fear in her eyes.

'What?' she said.

'You can sleep on my couch, Snow,' Moore said. 'And I might even cook you my famous spaghetti sauce.'

Astrid stumbled out of the cabin and lost her appetite.

Moore's place was on the other side of town, and it took an hour to get there once they'd picked up Astrid's rucksack from the fleabag hotel. He'd given Campbell the job of checking to see if anyone had booked into the cabin recently, and she'd left sharpish before Astrid could talk to her. She couldn't remove the image from her head that Campbell was married, racking her brain to remember if she'd seen any signs at the apartment. There were no photos of a husband and no evidence of anybody else living there. It was a curious thing, but she dismissed it as soon as they got into the drive, thinking it more prudent to learn something about the man she'd be staying with.

'Are you a local to Bakerstown, Detective?'

'I relocated here five years ago from Washington, but I'm from New York.' He scrutinised Astrid through the mirror. 'I hear you were there recently.'

She glanced at the town as they moved through it. The buildings were a mix and match of different styles: shops which appeared to have been built not long after the Civil War, large and small houses, schools surrounded by giant metal fences, with a hydrant on every street corner. They drove through a market with the potent smells of fresh vegetables and a world of spices drifting through the car window.

'Have you been checking up on me, Detective?'

He stopped at a red light. 'You can call me Jim, and I'll address you as Astrid, is that okay?'

'That's fine by me, Jim. So, did you dredge through my past when I was a suspect in the Cruz murders?'

The slight rise in the corner of his mouth transformed into a smirk. 'What makes you think you're still not a suspect?'

The pain returned to her ribs as she laughed. 'Is that why you're not letting me out of your sight?'

'Something like that.'

'Didn't my former employers convince yours of my innocence?'

'I don't know what was said between them, but I saw some of your Agency service record.'

'I must apologise then.'

'What for?'

'For your future nightmares.'

He tapped his finger on the steering wheel and gazed at the traffic light holding them up.

'Far from it; it was an impressive résumé.'

She focused on his face and wondered why he didn't look at her while the car was stationary.

'So, are you going to tell me what you know?'

The light changed to green, and Moore set off.

'About you? We had enough to hold you for the Cruz murders, with the witnesses, fingerprints at the scene and your passport found on Caitlin with your blood on it. Yet, we were told to let you go. That instruction came from the highest office in the country. So I did a little digging on you.'

'I hope you had a big spade.'

She watched him fight against it, yet he couldn't help but laugh.

'I called in a lot of favours to find out you're some British spy, and our government is keen to keep your employers happy.'

'Do you believe I killed the Cruz family?'

His grin disappeared as quickly as it had come. 'If I did, you wouldn't be with me now. Even I can spot a frame-up when I see it.'

'So, why am I with you?'

'Because I think you know things about that night that you haven't told me.'

'You believe I've lied to you?'

'Maybe, maybe not. It could be you've forgotten some of what happened, possibly through drinking too much and the beating you took.' He gave her a long, hard look. 'And I'm hoping those memories will return to you sooner rather than later.'

She thought about that as he switched on the radio, finding a country music station he turned up to full blast. There weren't many musical genres Astrid didn't like, but that was one of them. She gritted her teeth through torturous tales about cheating husbands and tearful wives until they arrived at his place.

They stepped out of the car into a wide street bordered on each side by apartments and small houses. Trees and bushes lined the road; the silence surprised her. She expected dogs or kids to be running everywhere, but there was no one around except them. He led her between stone benches to a smart-looking residence.

Once they got inside, he gave her a tour: a compact kitchen, even smaller shower, single bedroom and a living room. The TV was so small she thought it was a leftover from the 1980s, while plastic flying ducks and a single picture of Elvis in his Vegas tassels costume decorated the walls. It was the last thing she would have expected from him.

She settled into the sofa. 'You left Washington for this?'

He spoke as he went into the kitchen. 'I needed a change of pace. And, contrary to what's happened to you in the last twenty-four hours, Bakerstown is a good place.'

'What attracted you to this town?'

He returned with two empty glasses. 'My mother's maiden name was Baker, so I thought I might as well see what it's like.'

'And what's your conclusion?'

'It's as good a place as any, I suppose.' He picked up a photo frame from the sideboard, a picture of him and a woman smiling at the Grand Canyon. There was a glimpse of the vastness of nature behind them, but the thing which struck her most was how happy they looked. 'As good a place as any to start a new life.'

'I guess there are plenty like this all over the country, small towns where the majority try to get on with everyone else.'

'True, but sometimes sacrifices have to be made to keep others safe.'

'Of course; that's what made you an Officer of the Law, that ability to put yourself on the line, to put your body in harm's way, to protect those around you.'

'Protect and serve,' he said as he placed the photo down. 'Is that what you did in Britain?'

'Most of the time. There are things I've done which I'm

not proud of, but I suppose most people could say the same thing.'

'You were good at what you did?'

'I like to think so.'

She watched him scrutinise her. 'Are you allowed to talk about any of it?'

'Sure, but I'd have to kill you after.'

He laughed out loud. 'I'll risk it. Tell me something interesting about what you did as a British spy.'

'First off, I wasn't a spy. I was a problem solver.'

'A human-computer?'

It was her turn to laugh. 'Not quite. In these days of mass media information overload, some people crave simple solutions to the world's problems; unfortunately, there aren't many. This creates a perfect opportunity for opportunists to jump in and point the finger of blame at others and mislead with a few slogans. It's easy to do when the mainstream news has been dumbing down for decades, reducing complex situations to sensational headlines with little depth or nuance behind them. And the multitude of disinformation and outright lies on the internet, often from elected officials, only makes things worse.'

'I wouldn't disagree with that, but you said you were a problem solver.'

Astrid took a long look at Moore and told him something she'd told no one outside of the Agency.

'I worked an assignment once in a country holding an election in which a corrupt president was standing for re-election. He was a crooked businessman who had raided the central bank, installed his family to senior positions in his government, paid no tax and allowed his cronies to avoid it, and wouldn't tolerate anything but uncritical praise from the media. His primary tactic to get re-elected was to have members of his party ride around towns and villages, offering bribes from the money he'd stolen from the bank to anyone who voted for him. The ploy worked, and he won by a landslide.

'Do you think his supporters deserved to win, and people were right to back him because they had more than they did before voting for him? Or were they idiots being bribed with their own money to vote for a gangster?'

He let out a long sigh. 'You don't ask simple questions, do you?'

'You wanted to know.'

'So why did you leave?'

'Sometimes you get sick of all the lies and deceit and have to find something else in life before you lose everything which makes you real.'

'And you've found that on the back roads of America?'

America was a distraction, but she wouldn't tell him that.

'I'm on holiday. What's important to me is in England, and I'll return there soon enough.'

But return to what? If Courtney won't speak to me, how will I ever get to see Olivia again?

'I think you need a drink before any of that.' He moved towards a sideboard and opened it. 'What do you fancy?'

'A bourbon and Coke if you have it.'

He went into the kitchen, and she heard the fridge open and close. He returned with two cans featuring a cartoon bear on them.

'You don't want to try a local brew?'

She curled her lips and grimaced. 'Not if that's the same stuff I had in the bar. I think that's what made me ill. I know Americans are no good at brewing beer, but that was gut rot of the first order.'

He screwed up his face at her. 'America has a long heritage of quality brewing, and the Bakerstown Brewery has a nationwide reputation for excellence.'

'Is the brewery the main building in town?'

He nodded. 'The largest and the most important. It shut down for a month earlier in the year because of an accident, and most of the workers had to take unpaid leave. That wasn't good for the community.'

'It's the town's biggest employer?'

'By a large margin. If we lost that, the town would be in dire straits.'

'What was the accident?'

Darkness clouded his face. 'There was an equipment failure, and two people died. That's the most who have passed away in a single incident since I moved here.'

'Until I arrived.' He didn't reply to that. 'Were the police involved?'

'We were, but not me. Some machinery overheated and exploded. They were lucky more didn't die.' He held the can of beer towards her. 'Are you sure you don't want one?'

'No, thanks. The bourbon will do.'

He put the cans on the side, and she watched him pour the drinks as she scanned his DVD collection, which was full of true crime documentaries and nothing else. She shook her head and turned to the books on the shelves, which were all crime fiction and thrillers. The microwave tinged in the kitchen, and he went for the food.

Did I eat in the bar last night? No, that's why I got drunk so quickly.

Jim returned and placed a plate of spaghetti and meatballs on the table next to her. Then he poured them a glass of wine each.

Is this his seduction technique, to ply me with booze?

She was going to warn him about boundaries when he spoke. 'Wine for the meal, bourbon as an *apéritif*.' He downed his in one go.

She laughed. '*Apéritif*? You're posher than you seem, Detective Moore.'

He shook his head while she finished her bourbon. 'My neighbourhood was poor, a lot of welfare recipients, single parents, and crime. Big drug trade. My father was in the military, but he died when I was five. My mom brought me up on her own. We lived on food stamps. I did okay at school, not great, but not terrible, and decided I'd only have a future if I became a cop. So I did. I worked. My mom died, and then I met Lisa. We had a daughter. I thought all was good, and perhaps it was for a while, but somewhere along the line, it all went to shit, and here I am now.'

Astrid guessed Lisa was the woman in the photo. She didn't ask what had happened between them; if he wanted to talk about it, he would. Plus, she'd had enough damaging relationships in her past to understand why he wouldn't want to expand upon what he'd told her.

'And here you are in Bakerstown when you could have gone anywhere.'

'Things are good here, especially when you consider some other towns around here.'

'Such as?'

He didn't hesitate with a reply. 'Like Morton to the north and Sugar Hill east of that.' She thought he might show her where they were on a map, but he didn't. 'The prescription opioid epidemic blights both places so much, they're known for miles around as the Twin Pills. There are more dodgy televangelists than you could shake a cross at in those towns, each of them dotted with personal injury lawyers, touting for business with slogans such as, "Been in a wreck and need a check?" In Morton, the owners converted one of the town's only two hotels into a drug rehab centre.'

'Crime is one of the few human constants, Jim. It's what keeps you in a job and stops me from getting bored.'

'Speaking of which, what do you think got these five people killed?'

She twisted the pasta around the fork, and then slipped it into her mouth. It warmed the roof of her palate, but was a taste sensation, bursting with the flavours of garlic and herbs. She ignored the heat and scooped a second between her lips. She gulped it down before replying.

'You said the police found the paper in the mouths of Caitlin and her children; was each piece on their tongues, or right at the backs of their throats?'

He munched on spaghetti and spoke at the same time. 'It was as if they were about to swallow the paper when someone killed them. Do you think that's important?'

'My guess is the killer or killers murdered Cruz and her kids because of something she knew. And it's connected to the numbers and what they led to. Her helping me after the fight outside the bar gave them the perfect opportunity to cover up the murders. That was their second mistake.'

Moore sipped at his wine. 'What was their first one?'

'Not checking the mouths of their victims. If they'd found those papers, you wouldn't have a lead. If they hadn't put my passport at the crime scene, they wouldn't be in trouble now.'

'In trouble?'

Astrid downed half her glass. 'They're in trouble because they picked the wrong person to mess with.'

'You're not leaving Bakerstown in a hurry, then?'

She'd considered it and was close to leaving before

deciding someone would pay for what they'd done. Not for framing her, but for killing Caitlin Cruz and her kids.

'I'll stay if you want me to.'

Moore grabbed his drink and toasted her. 'So you believe it's connected to this human trafficking website?'

'That's the way it looks. It would help if we can identify those bodies in the cabin, but I doubt we will.'

'Why not?'

She finished her wine, then poured herself another. 'Because if they were locals, someone would notice them missing. The killer or killers destroyed their faces, fingers, and teeth to prevent identification that way. Unless...'

She dropped her fork into the spaghetti as a sudden revelation hit her.

'Unless what?' Moore said.

'Unless somebody silenced the two in the cabin because they killed Cruz and her children.'

Moore sat back and pondered her words. 'But why would Caitlin have those website numbers? And didn't you say there were three killers at the murder scene, two of them to hold on to the kids?'

'A big enough adult could've restrained them, so perhaps there were only two at the house.'

'Let me get this straight: you're claiming the two people in the cabin killed Caitlin Cruz and her kids because they were looking for those bits of paper.' He didn't seem convinced. 'Three pieces containing numbers which lead to a human trafficking website.'

'I'm not claiming anything; it's only an educated guess.'

He laughed. 'Which school did you go to?'

'Not one I'd recommend to any parents wanting the best for their offspring.'

Moore pushed his plate to the side, having only eaten half the food.

'Why didn't Cruz give her assailants the paper? She could have saved their lives if she had.'

Astrid shrugged. 'We have too many unknowns at the moment to guess why, but perhaps she knew her attackers, knew they were all going to die regardless of what she did.'

And maybe she tried to tell Astrid she was in danger, tried to warn her as she patched her up in the kitchen. Not for the first time since that night, she wondered if she'd let Caitlin Cruz and her children down.

Even if she hadn't killed them, wasn't she to blame for what happened?

8 LOOKING AT YOU

Astrid watched Jim's expression change, his eyes growing wide. Then he surprised her by changing tack.

'I thought you came here to find a grave? Is it a relative or friend of yours?'

He appeared to be making small talk, something she was never very good at. So she turned it back on him without answering the question.

'How does a big-time Washington Detective end up in a town like this?'

'How do you know I was a big-time Detective before I came here?'

'It's in the way you handle yourself, the way you move and speak. You have that restless suspicion only gained from years of questioning people.'

'I told you, I liked the name because of my mother.'

Something flashed beneath his eyes, a glimpse of a life she assumed he'd tried to forget.

'I think there's more to it than that, Jim.' She sipped at

the wine again. 'You don't have to tell me if you don't want to.'

He glanced at the photo, and then back to her.

'I was thirty years married and thirty years a cop. Then I find out my wife's been cheating on me for three years with my best friend and partner. Some Detective I was.' He raised his glass in mock salute. 'I'd say she left me, but Lisa kicked me out of the house, and I was a laughingstock with my colleagues. I searched for the biggest, darkest hole I could and ended up here.'

She'd heard many stories like it before, but there was something in his expression she identified with: a loss beyond control.

'You had a kid?'

He hesitated in response, and she scrutinised his expression, recognising what lurked there as a reluctance to talk about himself. She was about to steer the conversation in another direction when he answered her.

'I've got a seventeen-year-old daughter, but I don't get to see her much.' A grim shadow crawled across his face. 'Jenny lives with her mother most of the time.'

Watching the pain consuming every part of him, she was reluctant to continue talking about it. So she scanned the rest of the room and settled on his impressive LP collection, filling three long shelves.

'Is your music in alphabetical order?'

She was relieved to see a sparkle return to his eyes.

'Of course it is. How else would you store them?'

Astrid laughed as she stood and checked the records. 'I never know with you Yanks. You've mutilated the English language so much, you might have abandoned the alphabet completely and organised them by spine colour.'

Jim shook his head and got up, moving to the middle of

the first row and picking out a record at random. He held it out for her to see, a live album by Nico.

'Everything in its right place, Astrid.'

She took it from him and scanned the track listing on the back cover.

'Does that only apply to inanimate objects, or people as well?'

'What does that mean?'

She removed the vinyl from the sleeve and searched for a record player, finding it in the far corner of the room. He nodded towards it, granting permission for her to drop the needle on the record. She moved to the sound system and switched it on, replying to his question as she set everything up.

'Did you know there are hospitals in certain parts of the world where all newborn babies are entered into a database and identified by numbers and names?'

He rolled his eyes at her. 'Most countries have used an alphanumerical system as part of personal identification for decades. Passports, drivers' licences, ID cards and national insurance numbers are only a few examples.'

'As far as I'm aware, Detective Moore, none of those start at birth.'

Jim pursed his lips as Nico sang about a marble index. 'You've seen evidence of this, then, on your spy missions across the globe?'

'Perhaps. Or maybe it's only an urban myth to confuse the masses, like tales of lizard people and the Illuminati stealing the world's children for their evil cravings.'

He didn't seem amused by her words. 'Groups of perverts abduct kids every day of the week all over the world.'

'Kidnapping.'

'What?'

'If someone takes a kid, it's kidnapping. Abduction is when it's an adult.'

He shook his head at her. 'You're using semantics with me now?' He increased the volume on the music centre just as Nico warbled about waiting for the man. 'And you said we murdered the English language.'

It was Astrid's turn to shake her head. 'Well, you can't spell a lot of the words, can you?'

'We've simplified the language, made it easier for everyone by getting rid of superfluous letters.'

Her laugh tickled her bruised ribs. 'Get you with the big word. Superfluous indeed.'

Astrid's enjoyment surprised her. She scanned the record sleeves as the music filled the room. The sound quality was as good as anything she'd heard, and she wondered if Jim's sound system had cost him a month's wages.

'Everything about you Brits confuses me.'

Astrid examined the rest of his collection. 'In what way?'

'Well, are you English or British?'

'I'm both. England is a nation-state within the United Kingdom of Great Britain and Ireland.'

'But isn't there two Irelands?'

She laughed again and wondered if he was messing with her. 'I'll explain this to you using records from your collection.' She went to the front of the first row and pulled out a pristine looking copy of *Revolver*. 'The Beatles were English, from Liverpool.' She placed it face up on the table, then got *Let It Bleed* and put it next to the scouse mop tops. 'The Stones are, of course, also English, but from London, so your table now represents the north-south divide.'

He crossed his arms. 'Are you trying to wind me up?'

'Bear with me.' She removed two more albums. 'Here we have Tom Jones and Shirley Bassey, two of Wales's finest tongue warblers.' She put the Jones album on top of the Bassey one on the table. 'These two enjoyed some steamy tongue encounters of a different kind at some point, so we'll leave them together. Now, we go to Scotland.' She moved back to the collection. 'So, let's see what you have.' She grinned at the cover of the next selection. 'Why, Detective Moore, what do we find here?'

He took the Sheena Easton album from her hand. 'That's the wife's. She must have left it behind.'

'Okay, Jim, put it with the others as we get to the heart of the matter.' She pulled two more records from the shelves and gave them to him. 'Thin Lizzy represents Ireland, and the Undertones are from Northern Ireland.'

The Nico record finished playing as he looked as confused as she'd seen him so far.

'Am I holding on to these?'

'For now.' She collected the other albums she'd placed on the table. 'Great Britain is a geographical term referring to the island, also known simply as Britain. It's also a political term for the part of the United Kingdom made up of England, Scotland, and Wales, represented here by the records in my hands. It includes the outlying islands that they administer, such as the Isle of Wight, but I can't think of any musicians from those islands off the top of my head.

'The United Kingdom is purely a political term. It's the independent country that encompasses all of Great Britain and the region now called Northern Ireland, which you have there with the Undertones, because where Thin Lizzy came from seceded from the rest of the Union in 1922 to become an independent sovereign nation.'

While he peered at her as if she was mad, she removed *Revolver* from its sleeve and placed it on to the turntable. The music sprang from the speakers as Jim poured them both another drink.

'We'll have a bit of whiskey in the jar later, but how about we finish this bottle of wine first?'

She put the records down and took up his offer. 'You read my mind, Jimmy boy, and you have an impressive record collection, but I wish your lot had found my phone. There are thousands of albums on it.'

'I'm sure we'll find it, eventually.'

The tone of his voice told her it was unlikely as she moved to the window. The building was a large house converted into four smaller apartments, two up and two down. Moore had the first one on the ground floor and spent little time in the garden, from what she saw outside.

'This is the perfect place for people to disappear.'

Is this why I came here?

'You mean the ideal spot for someone to set up a human trafficking business?'

'Do you get many missing person reports through here?'

He shook his head and drained his glass. 'Hitchhikers and drifters appear at either end of the highway all the time. We could lose a small population that way and never know.'

'Have you heard from the FBI about the website?'

Moore collected the plates. 'I expect they'll be in touch tomorrow; if not, I'll ring them.' He glanced towards the bedroom. 'You have the bed tonight, and I'll sleep on the sofa.'

Her suspicious mind wondered if this was a ploy to make a play for her. He must have recognised the doubt in her face.

'I've been working so many shifts this last month, I

always end up asleep on the sofa. The guys down at the station call me a couch potato.' His laugh was supposed to ease her caution, but it didn't.

'No, it's okay, Jim. I like to sleep with my eyes on the door, anyway.' She grabbed a cushion and settled into the weary-looking furniture.

'Suit yourself, but be aware I'll be up at five.'

'That's fine by me. Hopefully, we'll have heard from the FBI by then.'

Once that was sorted, she'd be able to leave the town free of any guilt since she expected it to lead to the apprehension of those who killed Caitlin Cruz. There was still her brief romantic entanglement with Officer Eleanor Campbell to think of, but she didn't expect the married woman to have too many sleepless nights over her.

Jim dumped the plates in the kitchen and brought her a cover. He left her to settle into the sofa and closed the bedroom door behind him. She expected the bodies in the cabin to be identified sooner rather than later, and it shouldn't take too long for the FBI to find out who was running the trafficking website. With that information, she was confident even small-town idiots could put two and two together, especially with Moore around. There was intelligence about him which she rarely saw in law enforcement.

But what to do about Campbell? She'd call her first thing in the morning at the police station. She'd be leaving in a few days anyway, so did it matter that Eleanor Campbell hadn't been entirely truthful before they fell into bed? The conundrum rattled through her head for an age before she settled into sleep.

For the first time in ages, her night was uninterrupted by wayward dreams, and all she thought about was returning to England. The relaxation overtook her, so it was a full thirty seconds before she realised someone was standing over her. She rose to tell Moore to go back to bed, her hand up to give him a friendly punch. It was that action which saved her life.

The wire was over her head and aiming for her neck in an instant. Only it didn't reach there and cut into her fingers instead. Searing pain sliced through her flesh as the attacker pulled her towards him. Her blood seeped on to the wire and her skin as her hand gripped against the garrotte.

A Donald Duck mask peered down at her, and for a second, she thought she'd been transferred into a nightmare version of Disneyworld, a place she'd always wanted to escape to as a kid in that terrible house. The memory of her father's horrible smirk forced her knees up, so she twisted her side to bring her leg around and knee her attacker in the gut. He stumbled back and into the TV with a crash loud enough to wake the Devil. He didn't fall and sprinted out of the door as she tore the wire from her and threw it to the floor. By the time she'd scrambled outside, the would-be killer had vanished into the night.

'What happened?' Moore was at her side with a gun in his hand.

Stabs of electricity ran through her bloodied fingers. She held them up, so the scarlet glistened in the moonlight.

'Did you leave your door unlocked?'

The lines on his face stretched into one confusing point as he turned from her and stared at his apartment. She followed his gaze: the window appeared locked, and there was no damage to the door.

'I guess I must have,' Moore said apologetically. 'We'd better get you to a hospital.' He peered at her blood dripping on to the floor.

She used her good hand and pushed past him into the

apartment. 'No need for that. I only want a cloth to clean this up and stop the bleeding.'

He followed her inside, having the sense to lock the door this time. She was in the tiny kitchen, washing the blood from her fingers.

'Are you okay?'

'It looks worse than it is,' she said.

He opened a drawer and removed a bandage, wrapping it around her hand once she'd cleared most of the damage away. He threw the bloodied towel into the bin.

'Opportunistic burglars are rare in the town. I'll call it in now.'

Astrid held her hand up to stop him. 'Don't bother. I'll recognise those eyes when they try again.'

'Try what again?'

'This was no burglary, Jim; they were here to kill me.'

The certainty of it hit her at the front of her skull like a slow nagging hum.

His eyes narrowed. 'Why?'

That was the sixty-four thousand dollar question she was still trying to answer. The FBI was dealing with hunting down the trafficking operation; it was nothing to do with her anymore.

They went into the living room. It was five in the morning, and she guessed neither of them would get any more sleep. She searched for something to drink, hearing the clink of beer bottles as Moore brought one for each of them. The glass was cold against her good hand, the liquid chilling the back of her throat. She was surprised how refreshing it was. What she'd had in the bar must have come from a bad batch. That and the pain in her fingers made her feel alive and forget about the ache in her ribs. She pushed her face against the window. The sun would be up soon.

'Perhaps this is all about you, Astrid.' Moore slumped into the sofa where someone had tried to kill her. 'This Agency you worked for; do they have a grudge against you?'

She stared through her reflection in the glass and into the town outside. Was it true? Would her former employers have gone to all this trouble to punish the only operative to have walked away from their services? Since coming to America, she hadn't spoken to George, her mentor and leader of the Agency, but she trusted him completely.

'Something happened between that woman at the bar and me.'

'We know it did: she beat you up after you insulted her and the band.'

'It was more than that, Jim; there's something I can't remember about that night.'

He sat up straight. 'That's what I said to you. There's information in your head about Cruz you can't recall yet, but you will.'

Astrid sipped on her drink while he finished his. Then he went to get ready for work, and she registered for the first time what he wore: a pair of striped pyjamas looking like they came from the Ark. She'd slept in her clothes, and now her body itched like hell.

She tried to recall the events outside the bar while he showered and shaved, but with no success. Something lurked at the edge of her memory, a shadow beyond her reach, and it frustrated her. There were plenty of shades in her mind she kept confined, but she needed to bring this into the light.

He stepped into the room as she tried to resurrect that shadow. He'd changed from his nightwear into a smart suit, his skin glistening from his wash and clean.

'You scrub up well, Detective Moore.'

He brushed off her compliment. 'There's food in the fridge if you want breakfast. Then you should come with me to work; it will be safer for you there.'

Astrid shook her head. 'I'll go down the road for food. The fresh air will do me good, and there'll be no trouble when I'm around others.'

She had to eat before her mind could work, and she didn't fancy going to the police station yet.

'Tom's Diner is ten minutes from here, on the way to the station. We could go there together.'

'No, you go to the station and see what progress the FBI has made on the website. I'll walk there, see a bit of the town, and meet you later.'

He didn't look happy with it, but didn't talk her out of it. 'Okay, Astrid.' He reached into his pocket and handed her a key. 'Here's the spare to the apartment, and I've written my cell number on this paper.' She took both of them even though she still didn't have a phone. 'Have a shower if you want and ring me when you've eaten.'

She nodded in agreement and watched him leave. Then she went and had that shower, settling under the water and feeling the bruises on her ribs. There was no chance of her leaving Bakerstown now.

Someone would pay for what had happened to her.

And for what happened to the Cruz family.

9 NOISE NOISE NOISE

The sun caressed her face as Astrid left Moore's apartment, with her throat and ribs aching in synchronised stereo. She reached into her pocket for her phone, finding space and remembering she'd lost it during the fight. But she didn't need it when she could reach into her mind and resurrect a playlist from memory, selecting her favourite 1980s tunes. The sounds of *Ghost Town* by The Specials kicked into her skull, and she checked her surroundings.

The Bakerstown Brewery overshadowed everything as she strode down the Main Street, and she understood why the town's economy was wrapped up in that large, ominous building. Perhaps it was some of their brew which kick-started her on the way to the mess in the bar the other night.

Once she left the brewery behind, she reached an old shopping mall, empty that time of the morning apart from those workers limbering up for another day at the rat race. It was then all parks and wild spaces, a chance to enjoy nature and wallow between the large trees everywhere. There was a river somewhere, she could smell its freshwater aroma in the air, but she hadn't seen it yet.

After she'd left New York, Astrid's journey through America had been a welcome change from her life in Britain. She loved spending time in cities, they were in her blood, but having the chance to relax in a slower, quieter environment had helped to dampen the hyperactivity which had plagued her mind for as long as she could remember. Not that small-town Americana had turned out to be as calm as she'd expected.

She shook the thought from her head and reduced the volume in her mind as she entered Tom's Diner, finding a dozen customers there. It would be an exaggeration to say the place went silent and everyone stared at her, but there was a noticeable change in the atmosphere as she strode to the counter. A server with the weight of the world inside her eyes pushed a menu at her. There was no attempt to smile. Astrid scanned the contents and spoke to her.

'Bacon, sausage, eggs, toast, and tea if you have it.'

She wandered over to an empty booth next to the window, staring at the door. Behind her were a family of two kids and their harassed looking parents. Opposite them, a couple in their seventies devoured an impossible pile of pancakes. At the counter, two blokes constructed out of American steel and steroids glared at her through testosterone-fuelled eyes, and she remembered them from her previous visit: the ones who were upset she'd spoken to Angie Delaney. She counted down the minutes in her head before the trouble started.

Astrid peered out of the window, imagining the town a hundred and fifty years ago, a place full of adventurers, prospectors, thieves, and rogues. The Ranch House wasn't far from where she sat, maybe a five-minute walk. She pictured it again, searching her memories for what was missing from that night.

I drank too much, didn't eat, didn't dance, and got too wrapped up in that terrible music. And that's why I ended up outside in a fight with Stella Starr. That was it. Nothing else happened until Caitlin Cruz helped me; help which left her and two kids killed.

A different server brought her order over, this one younger and with a genuine smile on her face. It said Katy on her name badge.

'I've always wanted to go to Scotland.' She handed Astrid her cutlery. 'Have you been there?'

Astrid warmed her lips on the tea. 'I've visited a few times. You'll need a big jumper in the winter.'

Katy blushed and leant a little closer to her. 'Do all the men wear skirts?'

'Only the ones with the biggest thighs.'

She spoke through a mouthful of food as Katy slipped from the table with a massive grin on her face.

Astrid raced through the meal, savouring the bacon and fried eggs between gulping at the tea. She chewed as she continued to prod at the shaky memories in her skull, sitting in isolation as a stranger in a strange land.

She wasn't alone for long. The two slabs of cowboy beef from the counter stood in the place vacated by the server. The way they scowled at her, they looked like they'd give an aspirin a headache.

'Do you remember us?'

She put down the fork to look at them. 'How could I not? Every time I walk through a sewer, I'm reminded of your faces.'

They twitched in their spot, all nervous energy and

hyperactive eyes. 'We warned you once. You're not wanted here, girl.'

There was Astrid's favourite word again. She punctured the eggs and watched the yolk run into the sausages.

'What you want doesn't interest me, boys.'

'We kicked the British out, and we don't want you back.'

He had the voice of a two-digit IQ, the sort of man confused by anything which didn't sound and look like him. His mouth was writing a cheque his brain couldn't cash.

Astrid crunched a slice of toast between her lips before speaking. 'You guys fought in the Revolutionary War? That's impressive.' She glanced at the weapons holstered on their hips.

'Do we have to make you leave?'

They were taller and broader than her, and they had those firearms. She glanced around the diner, observing the rest of the customers with their heads bowed, their attention fixed on anything but the drama unfolding nearby. The staff had disappeared behind the counter, and she understood nobody was coming to help her.

But she didn't need any help.

She reached into her mind for her escape maps. Map one had her shoving a fork into the closer bloke's neck and the plate in the other's face. But that way led to the possibility of collateral damage and innocent customers getting shot. Map two had Astrid inviting her new friends outside for a more personal chat, but unless she stayed close to both, there was the chance one would fire at her before she disabled them. Map three was her doing as they said and leaving without finishing her food, hoping they wouldn't shoot her in the back in front of all the witnesses.

'We won't tell you again, girl.'

Someone famous once wondered why small towns were

small. From experience, Astrid considered it might be because it takes more generosity, neighbourliness, humility, and decency to live in one. Everyone knows who you are and what you've done. Folks who get above themselves, or get in trouble, or who can't get along, tend to move to the city where poor reputations and bad attitudes disappear in the crowd. But these two hadn't bothered to pursue that route.

She picked a sausage from the plate and stood. Astrid peered at it as if it was the worst piece of meat she'd ever seen.

'Why do you Yanks have such small sausages? They're much larger in England.'

She tossed it into the remnants of the egg and dropped money on to the table. Then she strode past them, never turning to see what they'd do. She held her hand on the exit door for a second, the cold metal of it cutting through the bandage covering her damaged fingers. Then she stepped outside, and the early morning sun raced across her face.

Astrid turned left and headed towards the police station and her rendezvous with Detective Moore. But there was something she had to do first. She strode down the street for five minutes until she came to the Ranch House, gazing at the neon sign of a cowgirl riding a steer.

What aren't you telling me?

She stepped around the side and to the rear of the building, hoping something there would trigger her memories of that night. She expected to find broken bottles and squashed cans, but the place was clean. It smelt of bleach and antiseptic and could have been part of the local hospital.

Astrid was about to return to the entrance when the noise of running water stopped her. It came from behind the barrels near her. She moved across to see what it was, surprised to discover a heavyset man emptying beer down the drain.

'Have you got a bad batch?'

No wonder the drinks from the other night made her ill. He turned to her, but continued what he was doing.

Is that why I got drunk so quickly that night?

His eyes narrowed and peered right through her. 'I don't know about that, lady. These barrels are out of date, so they've got to go.'

He continued his job, and she returned to the front of the Ranch House.

The hotel was two minutes in the opposite direction. That's why she'd ended up there that night, because she was too lazy to go any further. She remembered the place as a dive bar, and she adored dive bars.

The ones you love always hurt you.

Courtney had told her that when Astrid was thirteen. She knew it was a lie because her parents never loved her.

Perhaps another visit inside would jog her memory. The lights were on, so she went to the door and pushed it open. She took a deep breath, breathing in the fumes of the stale alcohol and dried sweat. The place was empty, apart from a pony-tailed hipster cleaning glasses behind the bar. He acknowledged her presence, but said nothing.

Astrid turned to find where she'd sat two nights ago. The taste of booze on her lips nudged her brain, slipping her into the booth where she'd drunk herself into near oblivion.

She'd got off the bus at six, found the hotel and booked her room by seven, then was on her first drink by eight. Then what happened? Astrid called the barman over with a flick of her head. He had large plastic circles covering both ears; they looked like he'd torn them from a shower curtain.

'We only serve hot drinks.'

'I'm after information. Were you working here Saturday evening?'

'Not me, lady; that was my shift off. But I've heard about you.' Biology had designed his grin to irritate.

'What have you heard?'

'You got your ass kicked by Stella.' His eyes were dirty brown, like rainwater clinging to the edge of a sewer. 'Then you killed a woman and her kids.' He curled his lips at her before returning to the bar.

Astrid dismissed him as soon as he left, the scene around him transforming into the night she was there. She'd closed her eyes and was back there then. The sound of the band playing on the other side of the room replaced the silence. Some shocking country and western tune about a bloke's broken heart. The place was barely lit, her vision adjusting to the gloom and the surrounding bodies. People argued or flirted in the shadows, while lonely souls stared into their drinks while positioned on their barstools.

She'd started on beer, some terrible local drink bearing little resemblance to what she was used to at home, before moving on to tequila. Perhaps it came from the hometown brewery after all. She'd tried one more time to ring Olivia, to speak to her sister, but there was no answer, and then the battery died before she could try again.

What happened to my phone?

The frustration had seeped through her that night, reaching a painful height when a couple arrived and sat in the opposite corner. She watched them arguing; only they weren't arguing as he was the only one shouting. His mouth moved up and down like a deranged kangaroo; his cheeks puffed out like a balloon as his skin resembled a blazing sun. She couldn't hear his words over the noise of the band, but she noticed how he squeezed the woman's hand as the colour drained from her.

Astrid couldn't make out their faces at first. The man tightened his grip on the woman's wrist, and she leant into the light, and Astrid remembered it was Caitlin Cruz, her face creased in agony. Astrid kept on drinking, never seeing him properly, but noticing the two skull rings on the hand transforming that pain to Cruz; skull rings she'd seen the following day at the gas station: Jimmy Sawyer.

She was about to go over and break those fingers when Caitlin stood and stumbled towards her. Cruz leant into her face, and she thought they were going to kiss. Then her hand was in Astrid's pocket.

That's where my phone went.

Cruz whispered something to her as she stumbled away. 'I'll not be...'

Astrid forgot about it at the time and kept on drinking. Then she staggered to the stage, and everything kicked off. Many people described it as a fight, but it wasn't because she never retaliated; she just stood there and took it.

Some words came back to her, what Stella Starr had shouted in her face.

'You'll pay for that.'

Astrid didn't know what the hell she meant. She was still laughing when the woman shoved her to the ground and slapped her head.

Astrid's memories of that night disappeared again. The next thing she remembered was waking up in that cell. Now she opened her eyes and stared at the bar, tasted the tequila, smelt the damp of the wood and pictured the skull rings of Sawyer.

Why did Cruz take my phone, and where is it? What did she say to me?

'I'll not be...'

It was two more words; Astrid knew it. Two words. A name. A name she'd heard again.

It was no use; it wouldn't come to her. She got out of the booth and left, wanting to ask Moore if the police had her phone, needing to see if there were any witnesses that night who saw her brief interaction with Caitlin in the bar.

Caitlin stole my phone on purpose.

If it had been with the victim, like Astrid's passport and fingerprints, the police would have used that to make a greater case against her.

So they didn't have it. Why did Cruz take it? To call someone without Jimmy Sawyer knowing?

The questions were running through her skull when a voice like nails on glass drove that thought from her head.

'We told you to leave town, girl.'

10 PRETTY VACANT

Astrid glanced up to see the two dumbass cowboys from the diner glaring at her. The silver from the handles of their guns glistened in the sun. A shaggy dog wandered around with its tail between its legs. She'd have sworn it was the same mutt that pissed on Campbell's car at the gas station. It must have been an omen.

'Do you really want to do this now, boys?'

She saw the excitement in their twisted eyes, witnessed their eagerness to beat on this female foreign invader in their town. Perhaps these were the next attempt after the thug with the garrotte.

'We told you to leave, woman.'

That was an improvement of sorts, the progress from being addressed as a girl to a woman. She stood outside the bar on the raised wood, two feet above them. A few other locals milled about, and she assumed they were hanging around to watch her get a beating again. She waited for the cowboys to make the first move; what she was about to do had to be in self-defence. But they weren't moving, so she gave them some extra motivation.

'Did you check your sausages to see if they measure up?'

The one in the white hat lunged at her. If they'd attacked together, they'd have had a better chance. She stepped to the left, catching him under the chin with the palm of her good hand. He flew backwards as if shot by a sniper, startling the dog, which ran away with a whimper. The movement shook the bloke in the black hat long enough for her to bring her arm around and strike him in his cheekbone. His jaw crunched as he crumbled to the ground.

She jumped down as White Hat went for his gun, stamping on his wrist as he howled. Astrid kicked his weapon underneath the wooden supports of the Ranch House. Black Hat got up quicker than she expected, grabbing hold of her damaged hand and squeezing more pain into her. He pulled her towards him and held her in a bear hug.

'There'll be no fancy moves now, girlie.'

His garlic breath crushed her nostrils as she thrust her head upwards, hitting his jaw and cracking teeth. Her skull throbbed as he screamed and released her. As he flailed around, she kicked him in the balls for good measure. When he fell to his knees, she relieved him of his gun and threw it with the other one under the bar. The people gazing at her from across the street stared in amazement. She waved at them and tossed her hair back, running her fingers against the bruise forming on the top of her head. The wounds were collecting on her body the longer she stayed in town.

'Thanks for the workout, boys; perhaps we can do this again later.'

She marched away from them towards the police station, obsessing about what had happened to her mobile and those words she couldn't remember.

IT WAS a hive of activity when she got there. Detective Moore was a bundle of stress holding on to a phone, while the other Officers did the same. There was no sign of the Chief of Police.

Astrid sidled up to Campbell and gave her best smile.

'How's it going?'

It's probably not the right time to ask Campbell about her husband.

Campbell's eyes were narrow, her cheeks shrunken as she flexed her hand as if about to lift weights. She handed Astrid a newspaper, which was still warm.

'The entire country went to shit overnight.'

Astrid scanned the pages. 'This isn't a hoax?'

Some of the most influential American institutions had suffered cyber-attacks: the Whitehouse, the Pentagon, NASA, Homeland Security, the CIA, and the FBI.

Campbell shook her head. 'Nobody's claimed responsibility, but the best guess is it's connected to the President pulling troops from the Middle East. Or it's the Russians again.'

'Which means our human trafficking website got pushed down the list of priorities.'

Moore stood at Astrid's shoulder. Pain zipped through her damaged fingers, up her arm and across her shoulders, where it nestled with the bruise on her neck and the fresh damage to the top of her head. She forgot where she was, stormed past him and grabbed his computer and keyboard.

'If the FBI can't do it, I'll find these people myself.' Her hands skimmed over the keys before he could snatch it from her.

'What are you doing, Astrid?'

'Everybody else's job by the look of it.'

Her hand ached as she stopped beating on the keys. He took the wireless device from her as the buzz of activity increased in the room. As she watched them work, she wondered if this was the whole of the Bakerstown Police Department. She did a quick count and got to twenty as Moore spoke to her.

'You'll need to clean this first.'

He held the bloodied keyboard up to her face. She stared at her hand and saw a sea of red. Moore dropped the plastic back onto the desk.

'Officer Campbell, can you please take Ms Snow to the hospital to get her hand fixed and then find her somewhere nice to rest while I do my job.' She tried to protest, but he stopped her. 'A little bird just told me what happened in town.' Then he returned to his work.

I guess news travels fast in such a small place.

Campbell took Astrid's healthy hand and led her from the building. She assumed the dizziness was because she was leaking blood and not due to the touch of the other woman's skin.

'The hospital's ten minutes away, then you can stay at my place.'

Astrid slipped into the passenger side. 'Won't your husband have something to say about that?'

Campbell started the car and it skidded off. 'Robbie's had to go back to Washington because of these cyber-attacks. He won't be around for a few days. Hopefully, we'll have this mess sorted by then.'

Astrid wasn't sure if she was talking about the murders or their brief dalliance. She focused on a simpler conversation.

'What does Robbie do?'

Campbell broke the speed limit as Astrid's blood dripped onto the floor of the car. 'He works for the Secret Service. Don't ask me what, but I guess it's something to do with wheeling the Prez's girlfriends in and out of clandestine meetings.'

She pulled her damaged hand into her chest. 'The President is a philanderer?'

'Even worse than JFK, according to the media.'

'He's single, so what difference does it make?'

Astrid had never understood why people were obsessed with others' private lives. The hospital lights flickered ahead of them. Campbell headed for the parking space closest to the entrance.

'This is one nation under God, Astrid. We're a Christian country, and the Prez represents traditional family values. If he doesn't satisfy his base, there'll be no re-election next time out.'

A cool breeze drifted across Astrid's face as she stepped out of the car. 'The country's under cyber-attack and the troops are coming home. I would've thought the people had more important things to focus on.'

'Sex sells, Astrid.' Campbell winked at her as they entered the hospital. Astrid's hand burned and tingled at the same time. The policewoman led her through staff and patients into a side room. 'I'll be back in a jiffy.'

Campbell returned to the reception. Astrid peered at the posters on the walls, warnings about drinking too much alcohol and sleeping with the wrong people.

It's too late for both.

The pain disappeared in her hand as she stared at it, seeing where her recent brawl had worsened the wound from the garrotte earlier on. She assumed it was improving until she realised the ache had only been superseded by the throb vibrating through her skull. Somewhere in the back of her head, the Specials continued to sing about a ghost town on a repetitive loop. Her fight hadn't been on the dance floor, but outside in the dirt of Bakerstown; she'd lost control, lost her phone and lost her purpose. None of that made her feel any better.

As she tried to find a new tune from her internal juke-box, creeping down a list of Birthday Party tunes, Campbell reappeared with a doctor who looked like a young Jane Fonda. Astrid sank into the medic's pale blue eyes, sitting back to embrace the stitches fixing her fingers. The doctor offered her painkillers, but she refused, needing to keep her mind as active as possible. She was barely three days into Bakerstown and had already had two fights, with one victory and a defeat, plus one unsuspecting attack. And then there were the things she couldn't remember.

How had she forgotten meeting Caitlin inside the bar, well before the woman helped her outside of it? Why didn't she notice her phone missing on the night, and why did Cruz take it? And what was the rest of the sentence Cruz had said to her when they bumped into each other?

She'd initially put this lack of memory down to tired-ness from travelling all day and too much booze, but she'd drunk much more than that before in her life and never suffered this type of memory loss.

What if someone spiked my drink that night?

That thought rattled through her brain as the doctor patched up her hand and checked her other wounds. The cuts on her fingers looked worse than they were, and the doc gave her some soothing cream for them. The bump on the top of her head was only a slight one and nothing serious, and she put a fresh dressing on her ribs. Her treatment was speedy and efficient, and they were in and out of the hospital in thirty minutes. Officer Eleanor Campbell kept schtum all the way through and as they left the building, so Astrid broke the ice.

'We should visit Maggie Delaney.'

Campbell stopped near the car, her eyes wide in surprise.

'You think she knows something about Caitlin's murder?'

'It's worth checking. If Caitlin spent time there helping Delaney, she might know something useful. There's not much else for us to go on at the moment, is there.' She felt like the walking wounded even though she wasn't moving. 'Unless you want to return to the station and help your colleagues with this cyber-attack thing?'

Campbell laughed and shook her head. 'No thanks, we'll keep away from that. It's bad enough Robbie's been sucked into it.' She opened the car. 'Come on; I know where the Delaney place is.'

IT WAS an ordinary house in an unassuming community. Some of the neighbours had American flags fluttering out front, but everywhere else was well-cut gardens and freshly mowed lawns. The sound of silence filled the street as Campbell knocked on the door. It was Monday morning, and they'd passed the school on the way there, but Astrid expected Angie to be in if what she'd said in the diner was true.

Campbell spoke before rattling the wood once more.

'Remind me why we're here again?' She didn't wait for a reply. 'Oh, I know, because of a hunch.'

A leaf drifted off the tree next to them and landed on Astrid's shoulder. She flicked it on to the ground.

'As an Officer of the Law, aren't you concerned one of your citizens is incapable of looking after themselves, and their fifteen-year-old daughter is staying off school to care for her mother?'

'We might be a small town, but we still have social services.'

'So, you can contact them if there's a need?'

'And you think that's the best use of both our time, Agent Snow?'

Astrid grimaced. 'Stop doing that, Eleanor.' The use of Campbell's first name surprised her by the look on her face. 'You're giving people the wrong idea about me.'

'And what's the right idea about you? Are you here to find justice for the Cruz family or to discover who framed you for their murders?'

'Can't it be both?'

Before it turned into a more heated argument, the door opened.

'We've got enough coal for now, thanks.'

Maggie Delaney looked nothing like the photo Campbell had shown her before they left. In that, she was a thirty-five-year-old with shoulder-length blonde hair and a smile as warm as the sun. Campbell had told Astrid it was taken six months ago at the Bakerstown annual carnival. The image was from the town's Facebook page. Now, on the doorstep, Delaney seemed ten years older, with a face caked in makeup and short hair shorn by Edward Scissorhands in the dark. She peered straight at Campbell's police uniform as she spoke.

'We're not here for coal, Mrs Delaney. I'm Officer

Campbell, and this is,' she looked at Astrid, 'this is Astrid Snow. Can we speak to you inside?'

Delaney's eyes shifted from side to side.

'It's about your daughter, Angie.'

This was the shaky plan they'd come up with in the car. Talk to Delaney about Angie's apparent truanting before broaching the subject of Caitlin Cruz. Officer Eleanor Campbell hadn't been happy about it, but was left with little choice.

Maggie Delaney's trembling fingers rubbed against her cheek. 'Angie? Is she okay?'

Astrid placed her hand on Delaney's. 'She's fine, Mrs Delaney. We need to talk to you about a friend of hers.'

So much for starting on Angie's absence from school.

'A friend of hers? Angie doesn't have any friends.' She pulled at her scalp. 'I've tried to get her out with other teenagers, but she won't. She's always stuck with her nose in a book or listening to music on that phone of hers.'

'Do you know Caitlin Cruz?'

Delaney's face lit up like a crashed UFO. 'Cat? Cat's my friend, not Angie's.' Her eyes sparkled as she shook her head. 'How silly to believe such a thing. You two better come inside.' She stepped aside to let them in.

'Thank you, Maggie,' Campbell said. Astrid followed her in, and Delaney led them to the living room. The place was spotless and smelt of lavender. Astrid ran her fingers over the sofa as she sat, noticing the lack of dust as she touched the leather. Campbell sat next to her as Delaney took the seat opposite.

'What's Cat been up to this time? Has she been upsetting people again?'

Astrid and Campbell exchanged knowing glances.

'What do you mean by that, Mrs Delaney?'

'Please, call me Maggie. I haven't been a Mrs for years.' Her eye twitched. 'Are you English, Astrid?'

'I am, Maggie. All the way from London.'

'How wonderful. I've always wanted to go to England, maybe meet the Queen and the Beatles. That Ringo Starr is such a cheeky monkey, but John's the thinking woman's dreamboat, don't you think, ladies?' She stared at Astrid before slapping herself in the head. 'Silly me, I should get you tea and biscuits, shouldn't I? You're English, so you must love tea.'

Astrid smiled. 'That's great, but before you do, can you tell us what you meant about Caitlin, Cat, upsetting people?'

Maggie stood. 'Oh, that's just our little joke. Cat comes here to work, brings her laptop, so no one knows what she's up to. She's always doing things online that people won't like, so she says, but she won't tell me what.' Maggie touched the side of her nose. 'This is the only place she has piracy, she says. Now I'll get those tea and biscuits.' She headed into the kitchen.

Campbell turned to Astrid. 'Piracy?'

'I think she means privacy.' She monitored the door as Maggie Delaney hummed *Paint it Black* in the kitchen. 'She doesn't know what's happened to Cruz and her family.'

'Perhaps she does, but she's forgotten.'

That was possible. 'Should we tell her?'

'I guess we should.'

As Astrid considered the best way of doing that, Maggie returned with a tray of biscuits, a small jug of milk, and a teapot. She placed it on the table in front of them.

'It's terrible what happened to Cat and the children. Is that why you're here?'

She poured the tea while waiting for the answer. Campbell asked a question.

'What have you heard, Maggie?'

'About Cat?' She dropped two sugars and a small amount of milk in her cup. Then she added four more cubes. 'Someone killed her and the kids on Saturday night.' She pushed a cup towards Astrid. 'I'll let you add your milk and sugar.'

Astrid picked it up. 'I'll take it as it is.'

Maggie's expression darkened as she spoke about the death of her friend. 'The rumour around town is that a stranger murdered Cat and the children.' She plopped two more sugars into her drink so that the liquid slipped over the edge and on to her fingers. From her cup, Astrid knew how hot it was, yet Maggie Delaney didn't flinch. 'Some English woman, I heard.' She wiped the tea from her hand. 'Did you bring any friends from back home with you to Bakerstown, Astrid?'

She ignored her question. 'What did Cat do when she came to see you? Are you a member of her church?'

'My goodness, no.' Maggie sank into her seat. 'I'm a life-long atheist. But that didn't bother Cat. She treats everyone with kindness, regardless of who they are.' The colour drained from her face, and Astrid wondered if she'd processed her grief yet. 'Cat would sit with me and we'd talk, and then she'd do her work online. Sometimes she'd bring Cathy with her, and she'd go off with Angie. Other times, Cat would use the house while I was out.'

Campbell sipped at her drink. 'Use the house for what?'

Delaney shrugged. 'She never told me, and I never asked. All she wanted was the Wi-Fi code and cold drinks in the fridge.'

Astrid drank half of her tea. 'Can I visit your bathroom?'

Maggie laughed. 'You make it sound like a trip to the museum, Astrid.' She glanced behind her. 'It's at the top of the stairs. You pay your visit while I chat with Officer Campbell.'

Astrid did just that, moving up the steps and wondering what Caitlin Cruz had got up to in the Delaney house.

11 SICK OF BEING SICK

The two of them were drinking their tea as Astrid went upstairs. She checked the bathroom, and then the bedrooms, unsure of what she was looking for. Everything was as spotless as down below, with that faint smell of lavender following her everywhere until she got to the last of three bedrooms. The posters on the walls and the shoes covering the carpet told her it was Angie Delaney's. A desk sat in one corner, besieged with jewellery, bits of cosmetics, and teen magazines. A few shelves were filled with paperbacks with titles she didn't recognise. Amongst them were some hardbacks she did, books about Hollywood and film stars of bygone years. She stood in the doorway for a second, questioning if she should enter and search the place. Her hesitation was fleeting.

She went through the cupboard and a chest of drawers, finding nothing unusual or out of place for a typical teenage girl's room. She checked over the books, flicking through a few to see if there were any hidden notes inside the pages. It was something she'd done as a girl, writing out her thoughts on bits torn from her notepad and placed in novels she knew none of her family would ever notice. *The Bell Jar, To Kill A Mockingbird*, and *Stranger in a Strange Land* were volumes her parents and sister were unlikely to touch, never mind read.

Astrid bent her knees and peered under the bed, finding old magazines and a few dirty plates and cups. Beyond those were crushed beer cans and the smell of tobacco. She got up and sat on the bed, running her fingers over the cover and staring at the movie posters on the wall. *Blade Runner* was next to *Dune, Chinatown* next to *Casablanca*. Some might have thought them strange choices for a teenage girl, but Astrid knew from experience that not all teenage girls were typical.

At least the kid's got good taste.

She lay on the bed, uncaring of where she was or who was downstairs, and peered at the ceiling. Her eyes glazed over as a long ache ran from her fingers down to the bruises on her ribs. The paint on the walls shimmered in a haze, and it wasn't Angie Delaney's bedroom anymore, but Astrid's from her teenage years. The posters changed to James Dean and David Bowie, Nina Simone and Diana Ross. All of them were youthful and in their prime. Astrid had never decided whether her favourite hairstyle was Bowie as Ziggy or Diana Ross's magnificent afro. As a teenager, she'd tried to grow both, receiving anger from her parents and ridicule from her sister. But by that time, she'd stopped caring what any of them thought about her.

At least that's what she told herself, then and now.

The bed also changed underneath her, becoming smaller and harder. Opposite it were her shelves stacked with books: volumes of all those places she'd transported herself to, better worlds than hers. She knew where she was, in Angie Delaney's bedroom, but her mind told her otherwise. The novels were now her collection of Asimov, Alice Walker, Stephen King and Sylvia Plath. There were DVDs and CDs on top of the books, things she'd accumulated from charity shops and car boot sales: Bogart and Bacall nestling next to Prince, Seinfeld rubbing shoulders with Laurel and Hardy, while Nina Simone pushed up against Au Revoir Simone. She was liking the synchronicity of the last combination until she realised she wasn't the only person there.

'You're always letting people down, aren't you?' Courtney stepped out of the shadows. 'Are you sure you didn't kill that woman and her kids, sister of mine? You've killed women and children before, haven't you, so three more won't make any difference. They're just more numbers to add to your ledger.'

Her sister's smile always had the power to unnerve Astrid, and it was no different now, even if she was a memory turned into a hallucination.

'Get out of my mind, Courtney.'

Her skull throbbed, and her voice sounded as if she was underwater. The figment of her imagination shook its head.

'Can't do it, little sis. I'm always with you, just like he is.' Astrid didn't look at the other shadow in the room. 'Plus, you understand you can't get rid of me if you want to be part of Olivia's life. You know this.'

Astrid blinked twice to remove her twisted vision, but it refused to budge. She resigned herself to speaking to it, even though she understood it was her subconscious listening to her.

'Do you know why you're blackmailing me like this, Courtney?'

Courtney smirked, a small pouting of the lips, narrowed eyes and tilting of the head.

'I'm trying to help you, little sis, like I've always done. But you're too good for us, aren't you, too good for me and Mum and Dad. That's what you've always believed. And that's why he had to discipline you, to control you. Otherwise, you'd have brought us all down even sooner than you did.'

Astrid grabbed her ribs as she laughed. 'I'm losing my mind. Either that or the beating I took did more damage to my head than I realised.'

'You keep telling yourself that, Astrid. By the time you acknowledge the truth, Olivia will have grown up, and you'll have lost any chance you had of bonding with her. Just like you did with me.'

She leapt from the bed and glared at someone who wasn't there, unable to stop herself from reacting.

'You're mad, Courtney. It was you lot who hurt me, not the other way around.'

The phantom of her sister pursed her lips as if about to blow a bubble.

'You turned Mother into an alcoholic, Father into a criminal, and left me without my parents. The guilt must be killing you.'

The ache in Astrid's chest went deeper than the bruises on her ribs. A steam train rushed through her, and she had no idea when it would stop. Her lips trembled as she spoke.

'Mother was an alcoholic well before we were born. As for him, Lawrence, I'm sure his sadism was steeped in his blood and bones long before he spawned either of us. As for you, I don't know where your particular malevolence origi-nated from, but I know it had nothing to do with me.'

The phantom Courtney Snow shook her head. 'Is it remorse which makes you lie to yourself, sis?'

Astrid knew what was coming, but still she asked the

question. 'Remorse for what?'

'You got Dad put away right when Mum needed him the most. What you did made things worse for us all, but more so for her.'

Astrid's legs wobbled and she reached for the bookshelf for stability, knocking a copy of *The Golden Compass* onto the carpet. The thump it created vibrated with the echo bouncing off the sides of her skull.

'You lie so much, Courtney. I don't think you're a good parent for Olivia.'

'How would you know, Astrid? You'll never be a mother, will you? Kids get hurt around you, don't they? Some of them even die horrible, painful deaths. At least Olivia won't have to worry about that.'

Astrid gazed at the vision of her sister and understood what she might do.

'I could take Olivia away from you, Courtney. I'm sure she'd come with me, and you're incapable of stopping me.'

'You'll never see Olivia again, Astrid. I guarantee that.'

The heat erupted inside her gut and sped through her veins. She dug her nails into her palm and waited for her vision to dissipate, but it took the phone smashing into her ribs to bring her back to normality.

'You didn't have to search my room for that.'

It lay at her feet as she stared at Angie Delaney.

'I'm sorry about this, kid.'

'Sorry for what? Going through my stuff or giving my mother a hard time.'

Astrid reached down and got the phone. 'Both. I'm just trying to find a killer.'

Angie's cheeks were redder than the sun. 'Have you tried looking in the mirror?'

'I didn't kill Caitlin Cruz and her family, Angie.'

'But you have killed before?'

I'm not getting into this discussion.

'Your mother's not well, Angie. You can't stop going to school to look after her. She needs proper care, and you need an education.'

'Who else will do it?' She stepped further into the room. 'I heard you talking to yourself, Astrid. I stood there and watched you saying those terrible things about your family. I don't think you're qualified to tell me how to care for mine.'

She's probably right.

'Do you know what Caitlin Cruz was doing in your house when she wasn't helping your mother?'

Angie crossed her arms. 'There are twenty dollars prepaid on that phone. You can add more yourself.' Her scowl was sharp enough to cut through steel. 'Now you and the cop should leave before I complain to her superiors.'

Astrid did as instructed and went downstairs to find Campbell and Delaney finishing the biscuits with today's newspaper on the table in front of them. She thought they were reading about the murders, but Maggie pointed at a different story.

'It looks like some of our boys are coming home.'

She handed the paper to Astrid, who sat next to Campbell and scanned the text.

'The President is planning to withdraw more than half of the sixty thousand US troops in the Middle East.' She understood how such a thing could add to the instability in some parts of the region.

Maggie Delaney poured herself another cup of tea. 'That will make the Hawkestra unhappy.'

Astrid and Campbell glanced at each other. The Officer asked Delaney the question forming on Astrid's lips.

'What do you mean by that, Maggie?'

Delaney started adding a ton of sugar into her drink. 'Cat would never tell me what she did on the computer, but I overheard her talking on the phone one day, and she mentioned how the Hawkestra were a secret organisation who controlled the world.'

Confusion spread across Campbell's face. 'Are you sure you didn't mishear her, Maggie, and the word she said was the orchestra?'

Maggie Delaney shook her head. 'Oh no; how could an orchestra rule the world? That would be just silly.' She scrunched her eyes and gazed into her tea. 'Unless it was the Electric Light Orchestra.' Her laugh fizzed around the room.

Astrid smiled at her. 'What did you hear Caitlin say, Maggie?'

Maggie cradled the cup in her hands. 'I listened to her on the phone for two or three minutes, and she said the word several times. I think the Hawkestra are hawks. You know, not birds, but people.' She placed a hand on her cheek, her eyes turning glassy. 'There were others, people opposite to them, but I forget who they are.'

Astrid pushed her spine into the sofa. 'You're talking about hawks and doves: Hawks are those who advocate an aggressive foreign policy based on strong military power. Doves try to resolve international conflicts without the threat of force. So yes, I could see why hawks wouldn't like the withdrawal of US troops abroad.'

Campbell seemed unconvinced by the idea. 'You think there's a secret organisation who rules the world called the Hawkestra?' She shook her head and laughed. 'I know you were a British spy, Astrid, but that sounds like something straight out of a James Bond movie.'

Maggie Delaney beamed at Astrid. 'You were a British spy? How cool is that?'

'That's not quite how it was, Maggie.' She turned to Campbell. 'Conspiracy theories of a secret new world order controlling the planet have been around for more than a century, from the Freemasons and the Illuminati, through the forged *Protocols of the Elders of Zion*, right up to QAnon and lizards in human flesh.'

'Lizards in human flesh?' Angie Delaney stood behind her mother.

Astrid smiled at her. 'That's a particular British invention and not from an old TV show.'

'Why would any of these nut jobs kill the Cruzes?' Angie appeared to have forgotten her anger towards Astrid.

'I'm not sure, Angie, but I intend to find out.' As she spoke, she noticed Delaney's fingers shaking around her cup of tea.

This conversation isn't helping her.

Astrid stood. 'It's time for us to leave, Officer Campbell.' She held out a hand to Mrs Delaney. 'Thanks for your help, Maggie.' They shook hands as Delaney beamed at her.

'It was my pleasure, ladies. I don't get many visitors, so it's always nice to have company.' She glanced at the clock on the wall. 'Still, Cat will be here soon, so I better put the kettle on. She spends so much time on that laptop, she needs a big jug of java to get through her work.'

Campbell followed Astrid out and back to the car. It had rained, and spots of water lay over the bonnet.

'Did you speak to the daughter upstairs? Because I heard you talking to someone.'

Astrid showed her the mobile. 'Angie got me this.' She passed it to Campbell. 'Put your number in it, and this is

Detective Moore's. Do the same with his.' She handed Eleanor the paper Jim had given her earlier.

Campbell added the numbers, then returned the phone to Astrid.

'What do you make of Maggie Delaney?'

'She's confused and has memory issues, but she needs to see a doctor for a diagnosis. There are many reasons for the way she behaved. Even if it is an early onset of Dementia, there's medication which helps with the problem.'

'You've dealt with something like this before?'

'I've read about it.'

'What did you make of her claim about this Hawkestra? You don't seriously believe in a secret new world order controlling the planet, do you?' Campbell peered at Astrid. 'Or do you know something from your spy work about this?'

Astrid held her mobile and messaged Courtney, telling her about the new phone number, trying not to think about the vision and conversation she'd had with her sister in Angie's bedroom. Then she sent another text, this time to her only friend in the UK, letting him know she had a new temporary phone.

Perhaps George is my only friend in the world.

She stared at Eleanor and understood whatever she felt for her now was only fleeting, and she'd be gone from this town sooner rather than later.

'I don't know what Maggie heard Caitlin Cruz say in her call, but there's no such thing as a New World Order. And even if there was, why would they kill a mother and her two children here?'

Campbell shrugged. 'So what's next?'

They got into the car.

'Did your colleagues find a laptop in the Cruz house?'

'Not to my knowledge. You would've thought the kids

had computers.'

'What about cell phones?'

'I assumed they did, but I'm not part of the investigation, so I don't get told these things unless I need to know or I ask.'

Astrid held her new phone and called Detective Moore. 'Were there any laptops, computers or cell phones in the Cruz house?'

'Is that you, Snow?'

'You don't recognise my accent, Jim?'

His gruff exterior projected itself down the line. 'Perhaps there's a British invasion I don't know about. Or there's more than one of you here.'

She laughed. 'I don't think you or this town could handle more than one of me, Detective Moore. Now, about that electronic equipment.'

'Give me a minute.'

She heard his fingers bouncing off a keyboard mixed in with his laboured breathing. Maybe he got little sleep last night. Then his voice shouted across the room with unmistakable anger rippling through the words, before returning to her.

'It's my fault. I assumed our expert had the devices and was working through them.'

'The police didn't find any personal electronic devices in the Cruz place, did they?'

'No.' That one word shot down the telephone line like a comet crashing to earth. 'Not even a gaming device for the kids. I don't know how I missed they had no cell phones on them or in the house.'

'It wasn't your fault, Jim, but perhaps they're in the same place as mine.'

'What?'

'Someone took my phone that night, remember?'

'What are you calling me on now then?'

'I got a new one.' Her laugh tickled her ribs. 'You're slipping, Detective.'

'Okay. I'm adding it to my contacts. What have you and Campbell done this morning?'

Astrid told him of the trip to see Maggie Delaney. 'She needs checking out by a doctor.'

'I'll organise a visit for her and Angie, though I guess the kid won't thank us for it. How are your fingers?'

She cradled the mobile in them. 'I'll survive.' Then she thought of something else. 'We need to check if Caitlin had any email addresses as well.'

Moore blew hot air down the phone, and she pictured his cheeks going in and out like a deflated balloon. 'I'll add that to my growing list. What are you and Campbell doing next?'

Astrid glanced at Eleanor, curious to know why the Officer hadn't told her she was married.

'I'm going to interrogate someone.' She ended the call before he could ask who she meant. Then she gave Campbell her widest smile. 'Are you ready for another clue, Eleanor?'

'About your mysterious grave in Rochester?'

'You haven't been cheating on the internet, have you?'

Eleanor scowled at Astrid. 'Yes, because I've had lots of spare time for that. Just give me the clue.'

'The woman I'm going to see once had affairs with Charlie Chaplin and Greta Garbo, but not at the same time.'

Campbell drove away as that thought collected with all the others in Astrid's head.

And somewhere in there, she heard her sister laughing.

'How long have you been married, Eleanor?'
Domestic bliss was an alien concept to Astrid. America went by them in a flash outside, great swathes of emptiness followed by trees and vegetation. They weren't heading to where they'd enjoyed some afternoon delight not so long ago. It seemed the policewoman lived on the edge of a forest.

'Robbie and I have been together for ten years. We met in the force, and then he moved into protecting and serving the few over the many.' Astrid detected a hint of disappointment in her voice. 'This used to be his parents' place until they passed away. I keep telling him it's too big and we should move into something smaller, but he can't let go.'

Astrid knew what she meant about the size of the house as she stepped out of the car. It was enormous, like three log cabins glued together with two extra floors above.

'What was that apartment we went to the other day?' Already it seemed like a lifetime ago.

'That was a friend's house.' Now she understood why there'd been no signs of a significant other there.

Astrid followed her inside.

'This must be a nightmare to clean.'

The lights were on when they went in. The place was warm, as if someone had left the heating on. Astrid saw a print of Klimt's *The Kiss* on the wall as they went into the living room. The house was bigger than a cop like Campbell could afford. The US Secret Service obviously paid more than their British counterparts did. Not that she was bothered or impressed with money, just surprised how well Campbell lived. It made their interlude the other day even more unusual.

Campbell closed the door behind them. 'Have the painkillers kicked in yet?'

Astrid was unsteady on her feet, hand reaching for the wall as they stepped into the living room.

'What painkillers?'

'I crushed some into the drink you had at Delaney's.'

'Are they sedatives?'

Eleanor grabbed her arm and led Astrid upstairs.

'The doc and I thought it best you got some rest as soon as possible.'

Astrid's legs turned to lead, her eyelids refusing to stay open. They reached the top of the stairs and Campbell took her into a large bedroom. She sat on it before falling.

'You didn't have to go this far to seduce me, Officer Campbell.'

'Perhaps later, Snow, when you're capable of consent. If you wake before I return, there's food in the kitchen and a bottle of wine in the fridge.'

Astrid was about to say something sarcastic when the lights went out.

IT WAS dark when she woke, disappointed to be wearing her clothes. Once the fog lifted from her brain, she felt great. She slid out of bed and flexed her bandaged fingers. Strength had returned to her hand. She wandered down to the kitchen and raided the fridge, taking some cheese and a plate of cold chicken into a large living room. She placed the food on the table, nibbling at the cheese as Caitlin Cruz's words came to her again.

'I'll not be...'

Not be what? What was it she didn't want to be?

And why haven't I told Moore or Campbell what I've remembered about my earlier meeting that night with Cruz?

She was picking at the chicken when she noticed the laptop on top of the cupboard. Astrid grabbed a chair and pushed it against the wall. She climbed onto it and reached for the computer. Dust swirled everywhere when she took it down, rushing up to her nose and into her lungs. She sneezed and coughed at the same time as she placed the machine on the table.

There was no cable for it, so she turned it on and hoped for a fully charged battery. The tiny electronic light at the front flickered through red and yellow before settling on green. She breathed a sigh of relief, running her bandaged fingers over the touchpad. She was amused to see the web browser's home page was the site for the Department of Defence and guessed it was Robbie Campbell's machine.

If he found out, what would bother him more? The fact I've used his Secret Service computer or slept with his wife? Perhaps they have an open marriage. Who am I to question them?

What she was about to do could get the Campbells and her into a lot of trouble. But she did it anyway. She cleared the DOD web address from the browser and typed in the ten numbers for the trafficking website, amazed to see it still active. Had the national cyber-attack stopped the FBI from shutting it down? She considered that as she opened another browser and searched for the domain name ownership and the hosting organisation of the site. It was easy information to find: the server was in Russia, which didn't surprise her. The person who'd registered the website name and transformed those digits into www.buyalife.com was one Jim Morrison of California. People really were strange.

She right-clicked onto the page to find the source code, scanning the HTML to discover anything useful. If she'd been at home or back with the Agency, there would have been hacking tools she could have used for this, but being out on her own made it more complicated. Tracing the credit card payments would take time and, she expected, would lead to shell companies and dead ends.

Astrid settled into the chair and finished the rest of the food. If she took the next step, it might lead to dire consequences for Campbell and her Secret Service husband. Hacking into the trafficking website would leave a trail to the laptop once the FBI got around to investigating it. She flexed her damaged hand and tried not to think about the hundreds of photos she'd seen on the site. Then she forced herself to picture those people, the motivation she needed to type in the code.

Little aches swam through her hands as her fingers danced over the keyboard. The Agency might have honed her hacking skills, but her education in that world had started well before she joined them. She put those talents to good use, though it took her forty-five minutes to break through the website's defences. Once that was complete, it didn't take her long to find what she wanted: the website creator's digital signature. She knew from experience most creators of illegal websites, even the worst criminal types, were too vain to leave their work anonymous.

It was a name she didn't recognise.

Medusa.

Outside the house, a large crack of thunder heralded an onslaught of rain. It battered the windows, screeching like harpies desperate to get inside.

She stared at the name again: Medusa. It had been six months since she'd travelled through the catacombs of the internet, and new people appeared and disappeared just as quickly in the underground digital universe, but she knew a guy who knew a girl who knew a girl who could help her. She cleared the tab and typed again, heading into the dark web, playing at Alice sinking through a looking glass that reflected the worst things in society.

She checked her dark web email account, deleting the messages one by one once she'd seen what they offered: plenty of hard-core illegal drugs; trafficked military weapons, including automatic rifles, grenades, RPGs, ammo, and body armour; stolen identities and fake birth certificates; hacked PayPal and bank accounts; counterfeit drivers' licences and phoney citizenship documents; forged money; bomb-making materials; and prostitutes or escorts.

The list of hackers was in a different place to the last time she'd visited, but she found it eventually.

Astrid scrolled down and settled on Phoenix. She figured one Greek myth might be in contact with another, and she'd employed Phoenix's services before. She sent the message and waited for the reply. Phoenix could be in any time zone anywhere globally, but Astrid knew how glued to their screens these hackers were.

While she waited, Astrid checked the rest of the house. The weather outside was apocalyptic; it was as if giant fists were battering against the building. She peered out of the kitchen window as raindrops bigger than plates dived into the swimming pool. If it carried on for much longer, the back yard would flood.

She wandered into the living room, admiring the Pre-Raphaelite paintings on the walls, with Dante Gabriel Rossetti hanging next to a John Everett Millais. A sixty-inch flat-screen TV stood at the rear, joined by an expensive surround sound system which she guessed connected to every digital device in the house.

There was a sizeable metallic coffee table in the middle of the room covered with glossy magazines. On two sides were shelves filled with books, everything from paranormal romance to high-octane space fantasy. Astrid ran her fingers across the spines, unsurprised to find thrillers mixed in with a selection of true crime titles. There was also a row of titles about US intelligence agencies.

She returned to the kitchen, but there was no message waiting for her on the computer. Astrid took a massive knife from a rack and sliced an apple in half; it was sharp enough to cut through bone. As she finished eating part of the apple, she received a reply from Phoenix.

The same payment as usual?

She used her good hand to type.

I'm away at the moment. I'll pay you when I'm home or will owe you a favour.

The screen was unmoving for forty-two seconds precisely.

What kind of favour?

Anything you want.

There was no delay this time, and the hacker on the other end of the underground digital world provided her with what she'd asked for. According to Google Maps,

Medusa's address was about an hour's drive from where she was. That surprised her; she'd expected them to be in the Middle East or North Korea.

She typed her thanks before logging out of her account. She cleared the web browsing history from the computer to save the Campbell's from stumbling into something they shouldn't.

Astrid reached for the knife to put it away, using her bandaged hand but not gripping it properly. It clattered to the floor as a massive dollop of rain smacked into the kitchen window. She bent to pick up the blade as something crashed through the glass. She turned her head, expecting an invasion by a branch as a grey circular object flew towards her and bounced off the table. She knew what it was before it hit the tiles.

Smoke erupted from the bomb and into the kitchen as she pushed her face into the floor. The bandage on her hand covered her nose and mouth, but she still smelt the stink of the gas. She didn't have time to gather her thoughts as two booted feet came into the room and her eye line. She recognised the material as thick black Gore-Tex nylon used for combat. Astrid gripped on to the blade, but if the intruder wore similar over their body, she wouldn't get the knife through the fabric.

She didn't know how many invaders there were, but there was no chance of escape while she was on the ground. It was a split-second decision, springing up to throw the other half of the apple at the guy's head. His reflexes were slow but automatic, his hand reaching up to swat the object away. Astrid knew it was going to hurt, but she had no choice. Placing her palm and damaged fingers onto the top of the table, she used its stability to swivel her hip and leap at the intruder.

Fuck!

Rivers of pain sprinted through her hand, her leg twisting in mid-air to catch the side of the rifle as he aimed it at her. The gun clattered to the floor as she landed and brought up her other leg to kick him backwards and into the cooker. His head caught the overhanging cupboard, knocking loose a square of flesh from between the helmet and his jacket. She lunged forward with the blade pointed towards him, aiming for that gap below his chin. That's when she stood on the apple and her foot slid from beneath her, her body bending one way as he knocked the knife from her. It clattered to the tiles as he grabbed her.

He thrust Astrid into the side of the table without slowing. It jabbed her in the gut below her bruised ribs before he twisted her around and pushed her into the cabinet. Plates and cups crashed over her and broke across the floor, following her down as she fell. A Laurel and Hardy salt and pepper set bounced off her jaw and added to her growing list of bruises, cuts and injuries. At this rate, they'd be replacing most of her if she ever made it to the hospital.

But that was the least of her worries. Her breath flew out of her as the trespasser dragged her up by the hair and tossed her across the other side of the kitchen. Her shoulder bounced off the fridge, and a group of magnets smashed to the floor. The man punched her damaged ribs, bringing his arm around and pulling her up again. The gun was in his other hand as she clutched on to a Batman fridge magnet and thrust the end into the gap in the mask where his flesh peeped out. She pushed it in as far as she could, like sticking her fingers into jelly.

Blood sputtered out as someone ran through the living room towards her. She reluctantly left the knife and the rifle to run to the back door. Bullets spattered around her as she threw herself into the rain. She landed on her shoulder, and a jolt of pain punched at her bones. Astrid rolled to the side and behind the bushes. The only light outside was that skimming off the top of the pool from the moon.

She peered through the gloom and into the mud and bushes, searching for anything to use as a weapon. All she found was an empty mug.

One set of booted feet landed next to the pool. She hoped there were no more. Her throbbing fingers pressed into the mug as he moved to where she was hiding. Astrid threw the mug as far as she could over the water, so it bounced across the pool and hit the other side. The gunman turned that way and sprayed the spot with bullets. She pushed up and hurled herself at his legs, sending them both crashing into the pool.

Water dived through her mouth and up her nose as she dragged him down. He writhed and kicked against her, trying to bring the rifle into her head but finding only liquid. She let go of his legs and grabbed at his throat, pulling off his helmet and staring into his panicked face. He was bigger than her, but she had the proper leverage, her knee pressed against his chest. As he grasped at his neck, she thrust her fingers into his eyes, feeling them explode as she dug her nails in deep. The liquid turned crimson around them as he thrashed against her. After about a minute, she let go and swam for the top.

She pushed her head through the water and sucked in oxygen, her lungs straining against her chest. She twisted to the side, expecting to see more intruders but finding nothing. Astrid scrambled out of the pool as noises came from the house. She didn't know who it was, so she rushed in the opposite direction, climbed over the gate and headed into the woods.

Astrid ran through mud and grass as the torrential storm pounded down, getting wetter than she had in the pool. The rain obscured her view, so she was unsure if anyone had followed her or not. Somewhere above her, the sky cracked in half, and the smell of fizzling electricity swam through the air. She swept damp fingers across her face, watching the bandage come apart over her hand. Bits of the material drifted from her bruised flesh and sank into the wet ground. Nature kept on hammering at her as if its sole intention was to wash her from the town.

She stumbled behind a tree and clung to it, the damp wood biting into her skin. Her breathing was laboured, her lungs fighting against the water trying to smother her senses. The branches afforded her respite from the weather, meaning she could see more than five yards in front of her for the first time since fleeing the house. Her feet sank into the soggy soil as she glanced down to see the worms struggling to the surface and wriggling over her shoes. Below her were the nightlights of the Campbell house. The rain lessened and she got an unobstructed view of the windows at the back, counting the shadows moving around inside; she thought there were two of them, but couldn't be sure.

Astrid pressed into the tree and discarded the last of the bandage, dropping it into the mud near her feet. She had no weapons, a painful hand, and the rest of her body throbbed like a fresh lightbulb plugged into a socket. Inside her overactive mind, she unfurled three maps for her current situation: run in the opposite direction until she found help, stay in the trees and wait for her attackers to leave, or return to the house to confront them. The final option was the least likely to succeed, but that also made it the most attractive.

Someone's going to pay for what's happened to me in this town, and I might as well start with whoever's in there.

She stepped out of the trees, her feet crunching through dead leaves and broken branches as the storm suddenly stopped as if an unknown creator had flicked a switch off.

Great. Now I won't even have the cover of nature to hide my approach.

It didn't deter her. She scanned the ground for the biggest branch on offer and scooped it up. She shook the dirt and the insects from it and felt the weight in her aching hand, already knowing the fresh stitches were falling from her fingers and she'd need to make another visit to the hospital once this was over, as long as she was still alive.

She stretched her legs as she moved, finding her feet sliding through the mud as she kept her gaze on the house. If there was a sniper there, then she was walking straight into a trap, and it would all be over in seconds; but she doubted that. The intruder she'd stabbed didn't have a rifle during their fight, and even if the two shadows she'd seen in the kitchen were people, they wouldn't have gone inside if they had rifles.

She was considering all the options when the ground crunched in front of her. Astrid lifted her makeshift weapon as the gun clicked five feet away from her.

13 DON'T CRY WOLF

Astrid dropped the branch into the mud. 'You know how to throw a party in this town.'

Campbell lowered her weapon and ran forward through the dirt and leaves. She clung to the gun as she threw her arms around Astrid, squeezing the breath from the soaking wet woman. They stood like that for a minute before she let go, and the colour returned to Astrid's cheeks. A red and blue siren wailed its way to the house as she flexed her hand, watching the blood drip into the mud at her feet.

Campbell holstered her weapon. 'What happened?'

Astrid stared at the damp cuts on her fingers and wiped rainwater from her lips. 'Perhaps someone doesn't want me staying with you.' Her joints felt like they had broken glass in them. 'Is your husband a jealous man?'

Somebody attacked me at Moore's apartment, and then this. What next?

Campbell frowned at her. 'Did you see who it was?'

Astrid shook her head as she peered at the figure getting out of the police car and entering the house.

'No, it all happened in a rush. They threw a gas canister

through the kitchen window and then forced their way into the building.' The smell of the gas continued to linger in her nose. 'They wore masks and body armour. There were at least two of them, but I think there were more.'

Campbell grimaced at those words. 'That sounds like the military.'

'Or perhaps the Secret Service.'

Eleanor laughed out loud. 'You're serious about this being Robbie's doing?'

'No, I'm not. I'm messing about to distract me from the pain, but let's see what's happening in your place.'

Astrid moved past her towards the back of the building. There was no body in the swimming pool, but the water was ruby red. As she entered the house, Moore was standing in the centre of the room, surveying the damage. His face resembled a fresh cadaver, with his cheeks sucked in and his eyelids drooping.

'Someone doesn't like you, Agent Snow.'

The way he used her name, calling her that, made her wonder if her former life was responsible for the attack.

Is this an old foe getting back at me? Somebody seeking revenge for my Agency work, starting right from the set-up with Caitlin Cruz?

She scrutinised the damage in the kitchen. Broken furniture lay everywhere, with glass and bits of plastic covering the tiles, apart from where the half of apple was resting against the wall. But the most important things were missing from the carnage.

'Where are the bodies?'

Blood spatters stained the floor and table, but there was no dead intruder, just a couple of overworked forensic guys dressed as if ready to go to the moon.

'We found no bodies, only lots of damage and blood.

Are you going to tell us what happened?' Moore stared at her as if she was his number-one suspect again.

She went over almost everything that had transpired after Campbell left her alone, leaving out what she'd done using the computer. Moore made no notes, only staring at her as she repeated the events of the night.

'An unknown assailant attacked you here, in the kitchen, and you fought him off. Then others entered the house, and you ran into the back, where you were assaulted again and ended up in the swimming pool.' As he spoke, Campbell's face turned grimmer and grimmer. 'And you think you killed him in the water?'

Astrid nodded. 'I can't see how he'd survive, considering I gouged his eyes out. I injured the one in the kitchen as well.' She scanned the room. 'There must have been more of them, and they removed the bodies before you got here.' Those were the shadows she'd seen, moving around inside.

She peered at Moore. 'How did you know about the attack?'

'My neighbours heard gunshots.' Campbell's voice was as shaky as Astrid's legs.

She left the Forensic Officers to their work and went into the living room, slumping into the sofa before she fell over. Moore and Campbell followed her.

Ten minutes' rest and I'll be fine. And I need some dry clothes.

'Did the FBI get back to you about the trafficking website?'

Moore shook his head. 'They're still too preoccupied with national security to worry about the abduction of innocent people sold into slavery, and God knows what else.' The whites of his eyes turned black. 'And now the fool has got everyone worried about some announcement he's going to make tomorrow.'

Astrid settled into the sofa and stared at the bunch of CDs she'd missed earlier. She noticed the collection of jazz discs on the shelf and assumed they were Robbie Campbell's.

'Who are we talking about now?'

Campbell handed her a glass of water, and she wished it was something stronger.

'The Prez is going to address the people tomorrow to calm everyone's nerves.'

'Okay,' Astrid said. Back in Britain, most of the population would go to the pub and get pissed during a national emergency; or people would evoke memories of a bygone age when the nation came together to fight adversity. As a kid, she'd watched her parents and their neighbours evoking the "blitz spirit" anytime a national crisis occurred, even though none of them was old enough to have lived during that war.

But she'd also learnt that the "blitz spirit" was an invention of the time, a government feat of propaganda to pacify a panicked and fearful nation, created with the best of intentions, but still a measure of how a nation's leaders manipulated those it governed. She remembered as a child flicking through a history book and finding a photograph of a milkman picking his way through the ruins to deliver the milk, projecting how ordinary Londoners carried on during the worst of the bombing. It was only years later she discovered the photo was a fake; the milkman was, in fact, the photographer's assistant, wearing a white coat.

Never trust what's right in front of your eyes.

She stood while Moore spoke to one Officer. She took

Campbell's arm and led her out of the room and into the corridor. 'Can you get me some clothes and a car?'

'You've had enough of this town? I don't blame you.'

Astrid shook her head. 'I have to do some errands, but I'll be back.' She felt the heat from the policewoman's body and smelt the jasmine lingering on her neck. She wanted to take her upstairs, but getting out of her clothes would only be so she could change into something drier. Eleanor looked about the same size as her.

'I need to borrow some of your wardrobe if that's okay?'

Campbell appeared momentarily confused. 'Oh, you mean something to wear.' She put a hand on her heart and laughed. 'Of course, go upstairs and take what you want.'

So Astrid did.

The main bedroom was the first she entered, admiring the large bed and the walk-in wardrobe. There were no photos of the husband and no evidence he spent time there. She searched through the drawers and closets, but found none of his clothes.

Perhaps they're in another room.

She didn't take long searching, settling on a pair of jeans plus a white shirt and blue top. A leather jacket lay over a chair, and she grabbed it as she returned downstairs. She'd transferred her phone, money and credit card into her new clothing and carried her damp clothes into the living room. Astrid left those on the table as Campbell joined her from the kitchen.

'Detective Moore is having a field day checking my swimming pool. I invited him to come back once it's cleaned out and Robbie has a barbecue.' She looked Astrid over from head to toe. 'You're welcome to come as well.'

Astrid smiled at her. 'Will your husband be confused when he sees me wearing your clothes?'

Campbell strode to her and ran her fingers over Astrid's arm. 'I'm sure he'll be able to tell the difference between us.'

'I'm sure.'

Campbell took hold of her damaged hand. 'You've lost the bandage, and the stitches have come out.' She touched the scar on the middle finger, and Astrid's vision went a little foggy. 'You must return to the hospital to have this fixed again.'

Astrid removed her fingers from Campbell's. 'It'll be okay, Eleanor.' She liked the sound of Campbell's name on her tongue. 'I can wrap a bandage around it later. There's something important I need to do first.' She glanced over the room. 'And you've got your hands full cleaning this mess.'

Campbell screwed up her top lip and appeared to consider her words. Then she examined the damage in her house and handed Astrid a set of keys. 'Here, take my car. I'll get a ride to the station with Moore. Are you going to tell me what you're up to?'

Astrid resisted the urge to kiss her, placing her good hand on Campbell's shoulder instead.

'You'll know when I do, I promise.'

She smiled as she left, glancing at the damage as she stepped outside and into the car. There'd been two attempts on her life, not counting the useless cowboys on the street, and someone had tried to frame her for a triple homicide.

Who hates me this much?

Her phone buzzed as she was about to start the engine. She hesitated as it vibrated against her leg, her fingers reaching for the car keys as the thump of her heart increased. Outside of Campbell and Moore, there were only two other contacts in her new mobile, and she didn't expect either of them to message her. The phone was for Astrid to contact them and not the other way round.

It must be from George.

George Cross, her only friend in the world and former mentor and boss at the Agency, was a man with strict instructions not to get in touch with her. But at the police station, she'd given Moore his number, and it was true she owed her freedom from jail to him. The Agency's influence would have been the only thing that could have got the murder charges against her dropped. They were the only people able to convince the American government to lean on Chief Colt to let her go.

The Agency: she'd left them, but still their fingers clawed at every part of her. They'd want something from her now, a favour for a favour. She sighed and removed the phone from her pocket, flicking her finger across the screen and entering the four-digit code. Then her face froze as she saw who it was from: not George.

Her sister.

Courtney.

She stared out of the window as Moore spoke to Campbell. For a split second, she contemplated returning to the house and pouring herself a strong drink before reading the message, but decided against it. Then she opened the text; it was brief and confusing.

Olivia is getting strange messages on her computer.

The first thing to cross Astrid's mind was why her niece even had a computer. The kid wouldn't be seven for another few months, so she didn't understand why she'd need one. Perhaps Courtney bought it for her birthday.

I'll never be able to compete with that. What, when I take her away from my sister like I told the phantom Courtney?

She was laughing at the stupidity of such a thought

until she realised she was only deflecting from her fears for her niece.

Astrid replied.

What type of strange messages?

As she waited for her sister's reply, she watched Moore put a consoling hand on Campbell's shoulder, and she wondered if there was anything between them that was more than professional.

The relationship between Eleanor and Robbie was unusual, that was for sure, and she hadn't hesitated in rushing into bed with Astrid. So who knew what went through Eleanor Campbell's mind? She pictured the photograph of Moore and his ex-wife enjoying the sights of the Grand Canyon and remembered the bitterness in his voice when he spoke about her.

She stared at the digital clock on the dashboard. Why didn't Courtney ring her? The next text came as she considered her question.

Olivia has a game on the computer where she plays against friends online. She's been getting messages there telling her how pretty she is, talking about her hair and eyes. And she doesn't have a photo attached to her account.

Astrid sank into the seat and slowed her breathing. It sounded like some pervert was trying to groom or stalk Olivia through this game. It made her heart sink while creating bile in her guts, but it was a manageable solution, even from where she was on the other side of the world.

She had to steady her fingers before she typed.

Keep her off the computer and go to the police. Tell them everything you told me, and they'll deal with it. Does she have any other access to the internet, through a mobile phone or at school?

The birds sang outside the window as she waited for the

reply. The wait was an eternity on her heart and in her head.

What if he's doing this?

She couldn't bring herself to say his name, but his grin lingered large inside her mind. And she remembered the other shadow during the vision she'd had at the Delaney house.

Our father. Lawrence.

As that terrible thought possessed her brain, Courtney's newest message arrived.

Olivia doesn't have access to a mobile phone, and she can't get into my computer because it's password protected. I don't know about the school, but I'll ask them tomorrow. Do you think she'll be okay?

How could she answer that?

Do what I said and keep a close eye on her at all times. Contact me again once you've spoken to the police.

She didn't say to call her, only to contact; she'd leave that decision to her sister. Astrid waited for Courtney to text her thanks, but she didn't.

She sat in the car for twenty minutes as a thousand different scenarios ran through her mind. All of them continued to linger there as she started the engine and checked the map on the passenger seat for directions. Now she was off to talk to a gorgon.

The tyres hissed over the tarmac as the Doors sang in her head. She felt the gentle rise and fall of the road beneath the wheels, crossing a bridge, and passing the sign for leaving Bakerstown. She was glancing out of the window and into a long stretch of countryside, until she hit a narrow space and the two cars blocking her route. The vehicle came to a screeching halt as she braked.

She was considering turning around when someone stepped out of the closest car. It was a bare leg stretching from the silver bracelet on the ankle to the edge of the skirt on the thigh. Even the sense of danger couldn't stop Astrid's libido from springing into action. It softened when she saw who it was.

Rosie Sawyer.

Sawyer swung out of the vehicle and sauntered over to the unmarked police car. She wore a tight velvet top which left little to the imagination. A glittering necklace caressed her throat as she walked. Sawyer smiled at her, and the night chill vanished in an instant.

'My father wants to meet you.'

Astrid pushed a fingernail into her thigh. 'Perhaps later. I've got to be somewhere else now.'

Rosie Sawyer removed a Polaroid camera from the silk purse on her shoulder and pointed it at the car. She squeezed the button on the front and took a photo of Astrid, who expected Sawyer to wave the image in the air, but she dropped it into her pocket instead. Then she moved a step closer to Astrid, aimed the camera into her face, and snapped another photo which joined the first one.

'It wasn't a request, Ms Snow.'

Sawyer nodded at the cars behind her, one of which spewed out her brother while the other contained two thugs, built like elephants with necks to go with it.

'I didn't realise I was this popular.'

Sawyer returned the camera to her purse. 'I'll return you when it's over; I promise.'

Astrid stared at Sawyer's legs before slipping out of the car. Rosie Sawyer gave her the sweetest smile before heading to speak to her brother.

'Stop messing around, Rosie,' Jimmy Sawyer growled.

'You go with them. I'll take her on my own.'

He glared at his sister. 'Father wouldn't like that.'

She laughed in his face. 'When has Father liked anything I do?' She was still laughing when Astrid got into the car and they drove off. 'Family; such a waste of space, don't you think?' Astrid didn't reply, gazing into the night instead. 'You're Astrid Snow, right? I'm Rosie, and that dumb lump of wood is my brother, Jimmy.'

Astrid found her voice. 'I know who you are.'

Sawyer's laugh was raucous. 'My God, I love your accent. I'm a massive fan of everything British. Here, look at this.' She reached across for the glove compartment just as the car bounced over a rock or a dead animal. Her hand flicked into the air, and then down onto Astrid's knee. She left it there long enough for a volcano to burst inside Astrid's veins. Then Sawyer flipped the catch to show the contents: dozens of photos lay next to a collection of David Bowie CDs.

'You've got great taste in music, Sawyer.'

'My stupid brother laughs at me because I won't stream any of this, but I like to hold something in my hand, don't you?' She took her eyes off the road and gazed at Astrid. 'To have something real between your fingers and feel the pleasure of it, to lift it to your face and smell and taste it. Is that what you like?'

Astrid coughed as the car lurched forward. 'My father used to have thousands of records which he'd spend hours with.'

'Oh, that sounds wonderful; so much better than digital files on a computer or phone. I've always known I was born at the wrong time. Does he still have his collection?'

The thought of Lawrence Snow brought Astrid crashing back to earth. Her flesh crawled as she remembered the danger she might be in with this woman and her strange journey.

'I haven't seen him in years. He loved my older sister but hated me. So he beat me until I ran away.'

She didn't know why she said such a private thing to Sawyer. She watched Sawyer's face turn to ash. There was a slight tremble on her lips, which vanished when the American spoke.

'If I'd had a gun when I was born, I'd have shot my father and brother on the spot.'

The silence was an abyss around them, a great big gaping void threatening to swallow the car and the world outside. At that moment, Astrid recognised a connection between them that went beyond the sexual tension, a bond forged before they were born into lives neither of them wanted.

Sawyer broke the quiet. 'Pick out your favourite album; we've got a way to go yet.'

Astrid pushed her broken memories aside and selected something more pleasing. She took the disc out of the case and pushed it into the player. The familiar sound of a train huffing and puffing drifted out of the speakers.

'How's this, Ms Sawyer?'

'*Station to Station*; an excellent choice. I knew we'd get on like a house on fire.' Sawyer's grin lit up the car. 'And call me Rosie.'

'I've never understood that expression. I've been inside a house on fire, and it's not pleasant at all.' Astrid stared at the back of the CD. 'Fire is a cleanser, perfect for redemption. Why does your father want to see me?'

Sawyer ignored the road as the car bumped over the potholes. 'He tells me nothing of what he does, of his operations and schemes. My brother is the favoured child. All I do is my best to annoy them.'

Astrid peered deep into the blue of Sawyer's eyes and sank below a sea of her own dysfunctional family values.

'Aren't you afraid to be with a suspected murderer?'

Rosie's hand slipped on the wheel as she turned to the windscreen and let out that breathy laugh once more.

'Oh, Ms Snow; I'm no more scared of you than I am of the wind and the rain.'

The car bounced from side to side as if they were at the dodgems. Their legs brushed together, and Astrid forced her heart to slow down. 'And I see driving wildly in the dark doesn't worry you either.'

Sawyer removed a hand from the wheel and reached

into her pocket, getting the two photos she'd taken earlier and handing them to Astrid.

'They should have developed by now. What do you think of them?'

Astrid peered at the first, of her startled face looking like a rabbit in the headlights. The second was more flattering, catching the blue of her gaze and her steely expression.

'At least you caught my best side.'

Rosie's laugh shook through her and rattled the wheel.

'Oh, I don't think I've seen that yet.' She winked at Astrid. 'But there's always later.'

The Thin White Duke sang about throwing darts into lovers' eyes as she scrutinised her companion.

'Are you a keen photographer, Rosie?'

Sawyer nodded along to the music.

'It's one of my favourite things in the world.' She pointed at the glove compartment. 'Put those photos of you with the ones in there for my collection.'

Astrid did as instructed and wondered what this enforced rendezvous was all about.

'Why am I here?'

Sawyer grinned. 'Why did you come to our little town?'

She rummaged through her brain to remember, to question why she stepped off that tattered old bus.

'I was looking for a grave.'

'Well, we've plenty of those.'

The night slipped away as a barrage of lights greeted them; there was enough illumination to guide a plane in as Sawyer stopped the car. Astrid got out and thought she'd stepped onto the set of *Gone With the Wind*. To describe it as a house would be to do it an injustice. She gazed at a beautiful white-columned mansion that crowned the hill they were striding towards. Enormous trees were on either side of it and nestled at their trunks were large birds. Off to the right stood another building, more modern and functional looking. Sawyer's brother and four goons waited outside it.

'I'm not getting a tour of the mansion, then?' Astrid asked as Sawyer strode beside her.

'Only presidents and governors get to go in there.'

A fence ran between the two buildings, and as Astrid stared at it, she saw how either end tailed off to circle the whole property. They must have driven through gates she didn't see in the dark. She followed Sawyer through the door and scanned the area for her bearings. If she had to leave in a hurry, she'd need an escape map ready.

It was built like a warehouse inside, with a top floor containing rows of machinery, boxes and barrels. They made for an office ahead of them.

'What happens here?' Astrid said.

Rosie removed an e-cigarette from her purse. 'We make vapes.' She cringed as she spoke. 'Father is wonderful at future projections. He knew before most others smoking was reducing in popularity, which meant there'd be a gap in the market for something else. Always have a backup, is his motto.' They were nearly at the office door. 'He told my mother he'd deliberately planted two of his seeds in her, so if the first one failed, he could use the second as a failsafe.'

'How romantic,' Astrid said as she walked into the room and stared at old man Sawyer.

Some people walk fast, and they talk fast, their teeth all chattering and jumpy as if they're going to fall out of their mouths. Benedict Sawyer was the opposite; everything he did was slow and languid. Not because he was old and his skin looked like rhinoceros hide, but because his mind appeared, she guessed, to work at a thousand miles a minute, and he had to force the rest of him to keep his thoughts in check. She recognised it in his black eyes and the way his mouth curled up like slugs sliding across the ground; recognised it in him because she saw it in herself.

'Sit, Ms Snow.'

It was a command, not an offer, crafted from a voice made from crushed gravel. She had no choice but to do as he said. The goons gathered around him like disciples at the Last Supper, all apart from Rosie who was standing next to the window, twirling a vape between her fingers.

Astrid waited for Sawyer to speak. One of the first things she'd learnt at the Agency was never to volunteer information. Silence didn't make her uncomfortable, but she knew most people would fidget, mentally and physically, if the vacuum went on for too long. As she waited for him to talk, she scrutinised the men around him: they were all tall, six foot three or four, as if they'd been snatched together from the same incubator at birth, and then stretched out. With arms made from solid beef, they stared at her as if she was the appetiser before the main course.

'Thank you for ridding the town of that irritating woman.' The words crawled out of his mouth. 'And I apologise for whoever did that to you.' He pointed at her hand. 'When I find out who it was, I promise to make them pay.'

Astrid flexed her injured fingers. 'You're happy because a woman and her two kids are dead?'

He placed his fingers on the table. 'Who am I to judge your actions, Ms Snow?' His grin curled her stomach.

'I never touched her or those children.'

'You mean, apart from inside the bar?'

'Why don't you ask your son about that? I recall him being there on the night.'

If only I could remember the rest of what she said to me.

Sawyer shifted in his chair as the son glared at her. 'It doesn't matter now, Ms Snow; all I'm concerned about is the future. I'd like you to come and work for me. It would be nice to have a fresh perspective on my team.'

Astrid stood and pushed her chair back, the wood screeching against the concrete floor. The thugs stuck out their chests in unison and flexed their biceps.

'I work for nobody but myself.'

The son bent his head to whisper into the father's ear.

'Ah yes, I've heard about you running away from your British spy group. And your family problems. I'm sure you could settle all your issues if you came and worked for me, Ms Snow.' She gripped the back of the chair. 'You could even bring your niece here to experience some genuine American hospitality. Olivia; is that her name?'

The blood drained from her flesh as Rosie Sawyer snapped photos of the people in the room. Astrid considered her options, calculating if she could deal with Sawyer's goons before getting her fingers around his neck. All the maps she'd constructed in her head led only to her demise. She consigned all of them to the bin.

'I need time to think this over.'

Sawyer's eyelids crawled over his eyes. 'Of course, Ms Snow, of course. Such a life-changing decision for you and your family needs careful consideration. My daughter will escort you to your car, and then perhaps you'll return with good news for me.' His smile made her skin crawl. 'And I hope the Campbells are showing you the best Bakerstown hospitality.'

She turned from him, blood boiling in her veins like lava. She left the building and marched out with an ache gushing through her bones. Rosie caught up with her as Astrid drew up a future map where she pummelled Benedict Sawyer against his vape factory. They got into the car and drove away.

'Would you work for my father?'

The car trundled towards the exit. Astrid saw the gates, ancient-looking metal constructs which slid to the sides as they approached.

'Why haven't you left here, Rosie?'

Her laugh wasn't husky this time, but nervous and low. 'And where would I go? I have nothing of my own, no money, nowhere to live. I've spent twenty-eight years in the Sawyer cocoon, smothered by people who won't allow me to leave.'

Astrid peered into the night. 'I ran from home many times, the final one sticking when I was fourteen. Then I lived on the streets before falling in with the wrong crowd and the wrong boy. I broke the law for them, and they abandoned me. Another group came to my rescue; eventually, I left them to be on my own.' She turned to Sawyer. 'You can't stay caged forever.'

They picked up speed, flying over the dirt and heading to the slip road where Astrid had left Campbell's car. Once she got there, it would be fifty miles before her meeting with Medusa. After an eternity of silence, Sawyer spoke.

'You don't miss your family in England?'

Astrid pushed away all thoughts of Medusa, remembering how Benedict Sawyer had licked his lips at the mention of Olivia.

'I have a niece I haven't seen for a while.'

Did Sawyer's reach extend that far he could hurt Olivia in England?

'It must be nice to have people you love,' Rosie said.

Astrid wiped the damp from the inside of the window.

'You don't know genuine fear until you've known love.'

It didn't matter what she found with Medusa, didn't matter who'd framed her; she couldn't leave Benedict Sawyer sitting comfortably in the knowledge he had something over her, not after he'd threatened Olivia. She stared at Rosie's reflection in the windscreen.

The road bumped a few miles more before they reached the car. They stepped out together, and Rosie took another photo of Astrid as she strode to Campbell's vehicle.

'Keep driving, and don't come back, Astrid.' Sadness seeped out of her voice.

Astrid had her damaged hand on the door as she turned to Sawyer.

'You'll see me again, Rosie; you and your father.'

She got into the car and put the events of the last hour behind her. She drove fifty miles with a playlist of Bowie tunes in her head.

And an image of Olivia in trouble.

15   FEEL THE PAIN

It was five in the morning when Astrid reached Sugar Hill, stopping at the first secluded spot she found. She wasn't tired, her mind wired by her recent experiences. She removed her phone and checked for new messages from her sister, unsurprised not to find any.

Did Courtney go to the police as I told her to?

Unless her sister had changed since they were teenagers, which she didn't expect, she guessed she'd wait until tomorrow before speaking to the police, which was a mistake. She read the texts again.

Olivia is getting strange messages on her computer.

Olivia has a game on the computer where she plays against friends online. She's been getting messages there telling her how pretty she is, talking about her hair and eyes. And she doesn't have a photo attached to her account.

Olivia doesn't have access to a mobile phone, and she can't get into my computer because it's password protected. I don't know about the school, but I'll ask them tomorrow. Do you think she'll be okay?

What Courtney had said was troubling, but she knew

there had to be more to it than those texts. For her sister to reach out for her help, it must be tearing her apart.

So why am I here? I should drop everything and go home. My family needs me.

Her ribs hurt as she laughed out loud.

Family! She hadn't had a family for a long time. She had no good memories of them, and her last visit with Courtney had only added to their mutual antagonism: a trip to her sister's house which turned frosty the second she arrived.

'You should have warned me you were coming.'

'I'll stick a red flashing light on the top of the car next time.'

It was the reception she'd expected, Courtney's face resembling someone who hated every reminder she had a sister. She made no effort to open the door any further than the few inches it was already. It was nine o'clock on Saturday morning, and Astrid wasn't there to heal a sibling breakdown that had festered for over twenty years.

'Is Olivia awake?'

Courtney didn't reply, stepping inside and leaving the door open. It wasn't an invitation, but Astrid took it anyway. She followed her sister through the corridor and into the living room. Courtney adjusted the volume on the radio.

Astrid sat inside this stranger's house. She examined the pale bare walls, the giant TV in the corner, the shelves full of porcelain figurines, and the framed photographs of Olivia. None of the furniture was cheap: a thick carpet separated a luxurious three-piece suite; two over-hanging lamps settled into the edges of the room.

'Olly is out with Jack on his morning run. They won't be back before mid-day.'

To Astrid's surprise, Courtney lit a cigarette.

'I thought you quit smoking when you were a teenager?'

Courtney snuffed out the match and dropped it into an ashtray. The cigarette lingered between her lips as she spoke.

'I started again when you began hacking for those criminal thugs.' She blew smoke, which swirled towards the ceiling.

'Can I return later to see Olivia?' The fumes attacked her lungs, and she fought off a coughing fit.

'Do you remember what I said to you the last time you were here?'

She twisted in the seat. Painful memories squeezed at her brain, obliterating her previous calm with the guilt sitting not on her face. but inside her heart. What had happened couldn't be undone.

'You said I was a danger to Olivia, and I should get as far away from her as possible. You promised I could phone her every once in a while, but that was it.'

Courtney continued to suck on the poison stick.

'Are you still a danger to her?'

Ghostly fingers clutched at her chest.

'I don't know, Courtney; I hope not.'

Her sister turned her back on Astrid, stubbing the cigarette out on the shelf at her side.

'Then I think you should leave until you know for definite.'

Without looking at her, Courtney reached over to the radio and increased the volume. Astrid stood and turned for the door.

'Can I still phone her?' Smoke drifted over her face.

'I'll get her to text you.' A smile crept from Astrid as she was leaving the house. It soon vanished. 'I've given Dad your number as well.'

Electric fire shot through her heart. Her knees weakened as her legs trembled. She stumbled down the step and into the wall surrounding the garden. A cramp stabbed her neck as she twisted her head around.

'He's alive?'

Courtney laughed at her. 'What made you think he wasn't?'

Astrid's fingers dug into the concrete. 'I was told he was missing, assumed dead.' She'd hoped he was dead, dead for a long time.

Another cigarette was in her sister's hand. 'He was travelling and incommunicado from the rest of us.'

'You've seen him?'

A thousand crippling memories crawled out of the sepulchres of her mind, horrible images that burnt into her sinew and muscle.

'He's here every weekend to see Olly; she loves getting to know her grandfather.'

Astrid wasn't a grown woman anymore; then, in the garden of her hated sister's house, she was young again: a child who all of her family had betrayed.

'You can't let that happen, Courtney; you can't.'

Her sister stepped forward, dripping ash onto the grass and spewing smoke into the air.

'You're going to tell me what I can and can't do with my daughter? What gives you that right, you who nearly got her killed?' The fire burnt in her eyes.

'He's dangerous; you know this. You can't allow Lawrence anywhere near her.'

Courtney lifted a hand above her shoulder and Astrid expected a punch. Her fingers trembled, but no blow came.

'You lied about him, and you ruined his life, and you sent our mother to the nuthouse because of it.'

She'd never seen her sister this angry. If she hadn't lost

all sympathy for her years ago, she could have felt sorry for her, but she didn't: the only compassion she had was for Olivia. Compassion and fear.

Astrid pulled from Courtney and left the garden. She strode away without looking back. On her flight to America, she'd wondered if she'd ever return home.

No, not home. Being with them was never a home. But would she go back to Britain? That thought lurked in her head until it pressed against her skull. She'd wavered, but these messages from Courtney would force her to return to England.

Even so, she waited.

She put the phone to the side and examined her surroundings. The town was built on a steep hillside with houses and apartments piled on top of each other along narrow roads. Streetlights flickered like fireflies as she scanned the area and registered the silent cars sitting outside the residences.

Astrid checked the address Phoenix had supplied against the GPS directions on her phone. The interlude with the Sawyer family had delayed her longer than she'd wanted, but she hoped Medusa was home. She drove a further five hundred yards, parked a block from the building and read the information Phoenix had sent: Medusa, real name Samuel James Morrison, twenty-eight years old, living at apartment 22b Parkland House, Parkland Street.

The night embraced her as she got out of the car. Stars twinkled in the sky, their flickering illumination serenading her as the jukebox in her head spun through numerous songs about nocturnal activities until she settled on her favourite Patti Smith tune. The noise helped her focus on her task, pushing the worries about Olivia into the far corners of her mind. They'd return soon enough, but for now, she relaxed and controlled the tension in her body.

The streets hummed as she stuck to the shadows and weaved towards Morrison's apartment building. Stray dogs chased each other on the street, jumping over homeless people and avoiding the odd hustler coming their way. It was the wrong side of the tracks, and she was glad of that. The more danger there was, the less chance she'd see the police, and the likelihood was reduced there would be any witnesses if anything got messy.

The more she thought about it, the less reason she saw for a connection between Caitlin Cruz and the human trafficking website. But those numbers in her and her children's mouths were the URL for that site, so there had to be a link somewhere. Hopefully, Morrison would have the answer.

She stood across the road and scrutinised the building; nothing appeared out of place. No lights flickered in the apartments, and no one peered from the windows to see her approach. She checked the rest of the street before crossing over, creeping up the steps and hoping the door was open. For once, she got lucky, pushing her way inside. The aroma of pizza and unwashed armpits lingered.

Her footsteps echoed through the empty entrance hall. A trembling overhead light cast a long, twisted shadow across the floor. Water dripped somewhere, creating a hollow oozing noise impossible for her to ignore. She assessed her surroundings, her eyes shifting past the graffiti on the walls and the abandoned needles near her feet. Everywhere was quiet apart from the liquid leaking on to the ground and the beating of her heart matching the music inside her skull.

There was an elevator in the far corner, but she ignored that and headed into the stairway. She pushed her way in, her eyes adjusting to the gloom and deciding no threats waited for her. She crept up to the second floor and through the door; 22b was the first apartment on her right. She reached into her pocket to find something to pick the lock before realising she didn't need it: the door was ajar. Astrid placed her hand on the faded wood and gave it a shove.

The lights were off, the small space only illuminated by the blinking street light outside the window. She twisted her head from side to side, scanning to see if anyone was there. She saw the bathroom and a bedroom, but her vision fixed on the person sitting in the chair at the far end: an unmoving body slumped forward as if asleep.

'Morrison, are you awake?'

Astrid didn't need to take more than two steps forward to realise he was dead. The smell of fresh blood hit her before she saw the mark on his neck. Somebody had cut across his throat and sawed through it. His head hung by a thread, eyes bulging from their sockets, the screen of his laptop flickering red and green as she stared at his corpse.

Bits of computer equipment littered the desk, with his blood staining the keyboard and mouse. She was about to search the apartment when she saw something impossible. Sitting in front of the dead man was the murder weapon, a piece of immaculate steel she'd seen before: the large kitchen knife she'd used to slice the apple in Campbell's house. And there it was, covered in blood and presumably her fingerprints.

She didn't hesitate, turning and heading into the bathroom. Astrid stuck the plug in the basin and switched on the tap. Then she grabbed a towel and returned to the dead man. She picked up the knife in the cloth and was back in the bathroom as the water reached halfway. She dropped the blade into the sink and turned the tap off using the cloth, making sure she wiped her fingerprints off the metal first. The blood seeped into the water as the sound of sirens drifted into the apartment from outside. The question now was whether to leave the knife there or take it with her.

Could it be traced back to the Campbells? It was possible, but if she took it with her and the police stopped her, it wouldn't look good. At least her fingerprints weren't on it anymore.

What if there are other things here with my prints or DNA on them?

She left the blade and returned to the living room. The sirens grew closer as she looked over the apartment; there was no time to check now. She opened the door and closed it with her foot, striding down the stairs and out of the building as the sirens advanced. She was around the corner and heading to the car when she realised what Sawyer had been doing with his little diversion and offer of a fake job.

He needed me at his vape factory, so he had time to kill Morrison and set this up. The job offer was nothing but a lie. But how did he know I was on to Medusa and was coming here?

And why was Benedict Sawyer trying to frame her for another murder?

The sirens were reaching a crescendo when it came to her: someone must have bugged Campbell's laptop. That was the only way they could have known. But how did they get the knife from the house? It was a crime scene when she left, and both Campbell and Moore were there with a forensic team.

She thought of the attack at Moore's place, then the one at Campbell's. Were they also in danger?

Astrid was contemplating the question as a baseball bat flew towards her head. She saw it just in time to duck, and it bounced off the wall behind her. When she lifted her head, she wasn't surprised to see the two idiot cowboys from the diner grinning at her; one held another bat, the other clutched a long knife in his hands.

They didn't follow me here; I would have seen them. They've been waiting for me.

The one in the white hat pushed the blade towards her.

'We hoped you'd make it back to the car.'

She glanced behind them. To her left was a large fire hydrant; on the right, a bicycle chained to metal railings. Would they attack together, or had they learnt a lesson from what happened in Bakerstown?

White Hat answered that by peeling from his friend and circling Astrid to stand between her and the kerb. Now there was one behind and one in front of her.

'You don't need to do this, boys.' She monitored the swinging bat and the pointed dagger. 'Whatever Benedict Sawyer is paying won't cover the costs for your stay in hospital.' Black Hat twirled the club above his head. 'If only you Yanks had proper medical insurance.'

They came at her together, the bat crashing towards her head as the knife thrust for her guts. She swivelled to the side and dodged their clumsy attempts, moving to the kerb as the cowboys stumbled into each other. They swore loudly enough to cut through the air as they bumped their legs and hit the pavement hard. She could have run then and made it to the car, but she needed information from them.

Why would Sawyer send two incompetents like this after me? Perhaps they murdered Morrison and left the knife to frame me, but they're hardly the brightest bulbs in the socket.

And what had she done to upset the man who allegedly owned Bakerstown?

They whispered something to each other and got up. The one with the blade laughed at her.

'You can dance all you want, girlie, but you can't dodge us forever.'

As they regrouped side by side, she stepped up and on to the fire hydrant, precariously balanced as they grinned at her like circus clowns.

'I'm not trying to dodge you, boys.'

White Hat smirked at her. 'What are you doing up there, missy? There's nowhere for you to go.'

'I wondered if you looked as stupid from up here as you do down there.'

She studied their movements, analysed each facial tic and curl of the lip, deciding Black Hat was the slower of them. In the instant she made that decision, they attacked with the bat and knife aimed at her. But she was quicker, kicking out with her leg to catch White Hat in the jaw and shatter his teeth, blood splattering the road like a Jackson Pollock painting. Black Hat's slower reflexes meant he missed her as she landed on the ground. She spun behind him and kicked into the gap between the back of his right knee. He bounced off the fire hydrant and hit the pavement.

Astrid watched them groan together as a small crowd gathered nearby, seemingly excited by the free entertainment on offer. Above her, nervous eyes peered through windows, and curtains twitched in the houses and apartments. The cowboys lay crumpled on the ground, scowling at her as she moved towards them. The baseball bat had rolled over to the side of the road, but the knife lay close to White Hat's trembling hand. She let him crawl for it.

'You touch that blade and I'll break your fingers, mate.'

He gazed into her eyes, and she imagined the cogs spinning slowly inside his head. He made his choice and pulled his hand from the blade.

'You'll pay for this, girlie.'

She sighed and towered over the two of them.

'Why are you here?'

Neither of them spoke, but someone behind her did.

'Kick him in the balls.'

Astrid glanced to her side to see there were more than a dozen onlookers. She didn't know who'd spoken, but it was a woman's voice. She turned back to her attackers.

'Who sent you after me?'

White Hat grinned through gritted teeth. 'Nobody sent us. We owe you for what you did outside the bar.'

She didn't believe it. White Hat was spitting blood on to the ground when she placed her foot on his ankle.

'You didn't come here because of what happened in Bakerstown.' They groaned in stereo. 'So why did Sawyer send two incompetents like you after me?'

Were they only delaying tactics sent there to stop her from getting back to town?

Why is he so afraid of me? Is this to do with Caitlin Cruz?

He'd called Cruz an irritating woman. Why was that?

Black Hat growled at her. 'You'll get your answer soon enough, girl.'

She was going to hit him again just for calling her a girl.

'And what would that be?'

The answer came from behind her before she'd finished speaking. Ringed knuckles smashed into her cheekbone, and she staggered forward and fell over Black Hat's legs. She lurched to the ground, her damaged hand no protection against the sharp thud of the cold concrete. Before she could lift herself, her new attacker kicked her twice in the stomach.

'That's because they were only the distraction, Limey.'

Jimmy Sawyer jerked his foot into her head before she could speak. His laugh was the last thing she heard as the darkness engulfed her.

Astrid woke strapped to a chair. Some tiny malevolent creature was stamping on her face while her stomach rippled with bruises. Sitting across from her was Jimmy Sawyer. The two cowboys leant on their baseball bats in obvious pain. To their side was a table covered with hammers, knives and other tools. She recognised a makeshift torture kit when she saw one.

Sawyer rubbed at the silver skulls adorning his hand.

'Before the government sent Pop to Vietnam, he spent some time in England. It was well before he met our mom, and he had a fling with some British whore.' He leered at her. 'I think that's why he's taking a fancy to you, girl. Or perhaps it's her he likes.'

He took a phone from his pocket and stuck it in her face. His aftershave made her gag, but it wasn't that which caught the bile in her throat. The image on the screen was a photo of Olivia. Not recent, maybe something off her sister's ridiculous Facebook page.

Astrid bit into her bottom lip and tasted blood. A mixture of fire and ice raced through her veins.

'Where did you get that?'

Sawyer pulled the phone close to him and ran a finger over it.

'I think Pop wants to bring her here, rescue the kid from the squalor you Brits live in.' His smirk threatened to consume Astrid. 'She's a pretty chatty girl, though. She'll do well in the mansion.'

A creeping horror engulfed every inch of her.

'You've been sending Olivia messages online?'

Is this what Courtney contacted me about?

He wriggled the phone in front of her bulging eyes. 'Don't they teach kids to be careful online in your shithole of a country?' The dumb brothers cackled behind him. 'How old is she, six or seven? We can get her ready for me in a few years.' He turned from her to look at the two goons. 'What do you think, boys? We could get ourselves a Jerry Lee Lewis thing going on.' He twisted his arms and shoulders in a macabre impersonation of dancing.

Astrid chewed on her tongue, using the movement to explore the delicate parts of her mouth; it was pretty uncomfortable.

'He doesn't know you're here, does he?'

He flashed those perfect white teeth at her. 'Of course he does, girl; Pop plans ahead for everything. He sent me here to check what happened to you in that geek's flat. I know he didn't want the cops to find you there. It was to stall you while he did what needs doing in town. We won't kill you, Snow. The old man wants you to come back and see him, but we'll have some fun with you first, won't we, boys?'

Sawyer kept the phone in his hand, moving it as he twisted his hips and legs. His body moved with a perverse purpose, like an eel squirming in jelly. He jerked around in front of her, performing an unnerving dance straight from a manic marionette's dancefloor. If that wasn't bad enough, what came next was even worse. He opened his mouth as wide as it would go and attempted something he must have believed was singing, but sounded as if a dozen cats were screaming their last. He continued dancing and placed his cell near the collection of torture tools, flicking through the screen.

Black Hat clapped his hands and spoke to his leader.

'Play some Rascal Flatts.'

She didn't know who that was, but guessed it wouldn't be palatable to her ears. Sawyer took the request and found the music. A weepy generic country ballad squirmed out of his phone and assaulted her body even more than Sawyer had done when he attacked her from behind. White Hat couldn't laugh through his broken jaw, but twisted perversion glistened in his eyes. Black Hat hobbled on one leg and pulled at the belt around his trousers. She observed them like an anthropological study.

'What's happening in Bakerstown while you're wasting time here?'

Jimmy Sawyer flexed his fingers in front of her, and she realised the rings he wore weren't all adorned with skulls. Only one set was; the others had small crosses on them. He held both hands out to her.

'God's love is being dispensed in town, girl. You'll get to feel it soon enough.' He pushed the skulls so close to her face, she smelt the dried blood on them. 'Hate and love, two sides to the story of the world. Sometimes we have to use hate to punish those who offend love, and your friend Campbell has sorely offended in the eyes of the Lord.'

Astrid strained against her bonds, hearing the sound of the wood creaking.

'What's your father doing to Officer Campbell?'

Sawyer grinned. 'God will punish the sinner for her many crimes.'

'What crimes are those, Jimmy?'

He stopped his manic dance and slid towards her.

'She sinned with you and others.'

He reached out to her, running his fingers across her cheek and down to her lips. She knew he wanted her to flinch, recognised this was him desperate for a reaction from her. Astrid didn't move, more offended by the terrible music than his touch.

'There's no bigger sin than that shit coming from your phone, Jimmy. Have you got any John Grant?'

He pulled his hand away before bringing it back with a hard slap, cutting across her face.

'Her sin is yours, English. Like with you, hers will be cut from her as she recants and begs for forgiveness. There's nothing to stop that. All we have to decide now is how to correct you of your evil ways, sinner.' Sawyer pushed the crosses up to her eyes. 'We'll have to force God's love into you from our bodies.'

She leant forward and ran her tongue across the silver of the rings, the taste of cold metal sparking her synapses.

'Caitlin told me you have a small dick.'

He flinched back and into the bench containing the torture weapons. Sawyer reached out, and his hand clattered into a large screwdriver.

'What did you say?'

'She kissed me in that bar. When she jumped from you and bumped into me, do you remember that?'

His eyes glared red like an atomic bomb.

'I saw the two of you, squeezed together and planning your sinful ways.'

She watched the control slipping from him as she flexed her body against the restraints.

'Caitlin begged me to take her away from you, said she wanted to know what it was like to experience pleasure, because you're so small she couldn't feel anything.'

The two goons hooted behind him as his face turned a delicate shade of purple.

'You're a lying bitch, and I'm going to gut you.' He squeezed the screwdriver in his fingers.

'Your sister told me the same thing about your dick, said she thought you were another girl the first time she saw you naked. Rosie told me all your father's men call you Tiny behind your back.'

Steam rose from his nose and ears, his skin turning redder than orange. He was about to pop, and she had to get the timing right.

'A world of hurt is coming for you, girl.' His hands shook, and she prepared for him to lunge at her. He took a step forward and she ran through the escape map in her head. But then he stopped and pointed the screwdriver towards her. 'Cat didn't say any of that to you, and my sister is a lying cow. Now you'll suffer for all your lies.'

'I'm already paying for it, Sawyer, having your stink in my face all this time. I mean, if you're going to do it, get on with it so these two cowboys can see what you haven't got between your legs.'

He growled as he thrust towards her, the screwdriver coming straight for her head. She assumed any thought of keeping her alive for his father had vanished in his rage.

She gripped on to the chair and leapt, twisting her hips, so the back of it caught the full force of his swing. It splintered against his arm, throwing her into the cowboy struggling on one leg while Sawyer continued with his forward motion and into the wall. She rolled over the bloke as he lay concussed on the ground and jumped up as Sawyer howled. The chair was off her back, but her arms were still tied to it. But at least she could move them freely.

White Hat's jaw was already on the floor, but she kicked him in the balls to make sure he wouldn't be a problem. He crumpled like a sack of potatoes. She stamped on his ankle for good measure, the crack of the bone making a pleasing sound in her ears. Now it was only her and Sawyer, him with his screwdriver and those stupid rings.

He swung at her again. She ducked, grabbed a broken piece of wood dangling from her arm and jabbed it into his thigh. He dropped the screwdriver and screamed. The fight was already over, but he didn't know it.

Astrid moved to the table and picked up a claw hammer. That would do. She used it to hit him in the nape of his neck. He fell on to the torture table and scattered the tools over the floor. She stepped over him and went to the cowering cowboys. They pissed themselves in stereo, two long streaks of yellow washing out of them, and she inched away from the stink.

'That's nice, boys.' She patted the hammer into her palm. 'Is my car outside?' They groaned and nodded together. 'Good. So which of you has the keys?'

Black Hat pushed through his pain and into his pocket. He fished out the keys and tossed them at her feet. She scooped them up and returned to Sawyer. She had one last thing to do before heading back to Bakerstown.

17   THANKS FOR THE NIGHT

Some of Jimmy Sawyer's blood still stained her nails as she drove away.

What she did to him took longer than she'd expected. She thought a big man like Sawyer would have been more stoic, but he squirmed like a stuck pig every time she went to work. Even with the double set of restraints Astrid used on him, there were times he nearly escaped from that chair. At least the gag stuffed in his mouth meant she didn't have to listen to his screams. And she'd changed the music on his phone to something more soothing than that country crap from before, finding an online playlist of Rolling Stones tunes. The only other sounds accompanying her were the hushed whimpers of Sawyer's goons. She'd left them untied, guessing right they'd be no bother to her. Two beatings had been enough to curtail any thoughts they might have had of attacking her again.

She didn't mind them observing her work. Her time at the Agency had included many moments when people watched her from behind two-way mirrors. What did trouble her was how much she'd enjoyed what she did to

Sawyer. And that's why it took longer than it should have. Every artistic move of her fingers swept away her worries about Olivia, about whether Courtney could protect her daughter. And even the lingering doubts regarding the involvement of her father retreated to the shadows in her skull.

But she'd enjoyed her time with Sawyer too much. It meant she was halfway back to Bakerstown when she realised she'd lost another phone. The one Angie Delaney had given her had disappeared from her pocket during her confrontation with the two thugs on the street, or they'd taken it from her when she was unconscious.

Astrid pulled the car off the road and slammed her good hand on to the wheel as the engine growled. She got out and kicked at the stones in the grass verge, her heartbeat increasing to match the thump in her head.

Fuck! Now Olivia can't contact me. Or Courtney can't.

She turned from the side and peered at her reflection in the car window. To calm her mind, she started counting the lines on her face, stopping after a minute before becoming too depressed. The wind whistled into the nape of her neck, the touch of it making her feel better than she should have.

I'll use Eleanor's phone when I get back and call Courtney. I can put up with talking to her for Olivia's sake. I should forget about Bakerstown and head home.

But could she? Didn't she owe Cruz and her children something?

It all started with Caitlin helping me. Benedict Sawyer's attacks were all because of that. Perhaps one of my former enemies is paying him to do this. It wouldn't be the first time.

So the easiest thing would be to pack up and return to England. That's what she imagined her reflection saying to her as she stood next to the car.

Go home. You made Jimmy Sawyer suffer. There's nothing else to do. The Cruz murders weren't your fault. More people will die if you hang around. They always do.

She pushed her damaged hand into the window, wiping at the other version of herself. Sawyer's blood trickled on to the glass and stuck to her reflected cheek. She turned from it and stared into the sky.

What did Cruz, the trafficking website, and Benedict Sawyer have in common? Who put those numbers into the mouths of the Cruz family? Did their killers do it? If not, why didn't they check the bodies and remove them?

She thought of the cowboy goons who had attacked her twice. They were stupid enough to do such a thing, but could they kill a mother and her children like that? And then there were the murders in the cabin. She'd assumed the victims had murdered the Cruz family, and were then silenced by whoever had hired them. But what if they hadn't; what if they were only another distraction?

Does this all lead back to Benedict Sawyer? Or does it all lead back to me?

Those thoughts bounced inside her head on the return to Bakerstown. The only thing to vanquish them was the sight of flashing lights outside the Campbell house.

A stomach-churning wrench grabbed at her guts. She was out of the car and running into the building when a paramedic stopped her. She looked around him, seeing two of his colleagues, but no police.

'I wouldn't go in there, Ms. It's not very pretty.'

She pulled from him as sirens approached and stormed into the house. Campbell was on the floor, brains splattered everywhere. But this wasn't her Campbell; it was the Secret Service man, Robbie. She recognised what was left of his face from the wedding photograph standing on the shelf behind his corpse.

'It looks like he shot himself.' The paramedic from outside had followed her in. 'Not surprising if he did what's in the kitchen. I've seen nothing like that.'

Astrid steeled herself for the sight. It was the smell which hit her first; she'd experienced it many times in the morgue and at autopsies, but never as fresh as this: the overwhelming stench of the contents of the human body rotting in the air.

She took a deep breath and strode into the kitchen. Even her hardened senses flinched at the sight: a body nailed through the hands and the feet across the top of the table. The same place where she'd sat not so long ago. The blood had congealed where it had slid to the floor.

She stepped forward and examined the deceased. Someone had taken a knife and sliced down from under the chin, not stopping until they'd reached the genitals. The murderer had scooped out all the internal organs and placed them around the corpse as if they were small plates of food on a tapas menu. She wondered if it had happened while the victim still lived.

Astrid dodged the blood and guts clinging to the floor and stared at the face of someone who must have endured terrible agony. But it wasn't Officer Campbell she peered at, but Detective Moore.

She moved back and pulled at her throat; her bruised fingers ached, while her skull throbbed. Her stomach churned and she twisted from the body, her mind returning to the last time she'd seen him, outside this house.

Why kill Robbie Campbell and Jim Moore? What am I missing? And where's Eleanor?

Astrid regained control and turned back to the dead

man. It wasn't only about killing Moore, but using him as a message or some example. Why else would they have eviscerated him and left the organs on the table?

Jimmy Sawyer and his two goons couldn't have done this because they were with me in Sugar Hill. So who?

The paramedic thought Robbie Campbell had killed Moore and then himself, but where was the evidence for that? Forensics would know for definite when they checked Campbell's body by examining the fatal shot's angle and the exit wound, but she went to look for herself.

The living room was empty, apart from the corpse. She didn't question where the paramedics had gone and stepped across to Robbie Campbell. She scanned the room first, searching for signs of conflict or an intruder. Everything appeared to be in its proper place, with no sign of damage or breakage. She bent her legs and peered at the remains of his face. It seemed to be an act of suicide from a cursory glance, but it was difficult to tell from where the body lay, and she couldn't move it. The last thing she needed was her DNA on him.

Perhaps Sawyer is trying to frame me for more murders.

But where was the weapon? She stood and rechecked the room, not seeing a gun, so returned to the kitchen. It wasn't there either, or the blade the killer must have used to slice up Detective Moore.

If it was a murder-suicide, at least the firearm should be in the house. Unless it was another attempt at framing her and the weapons would turn up with her DNA on them somewhere.

None of this makes any sense. If Benedict Sawyer or anyone else wanted me out of the way, they could have killed me easy enough, starting with the night I was that drunk, Caitlin Cruz took me home to patch me up.

She shook her head and strode out, not wanting to be there when the police arrived. As she stepped outside, the paramedic approached her again.

'Are you Astrid Snow?'

She hesitated, wondering what she might implicate herself in before her composure returned. At least she hadn't found Eleanor's body in the house. Perhaps this bloke had news about her.

'I am.'

'This is for you.' He handed her a cell phone.

She placed it to her ear, guessing who it would be. There was a long drawn-out breath at the other end before Benedict Sawyer spoke.

'Have you considered my job offer, Ms Snow?'

'I'm about to give you my reply in person, Sawyer. No amount of goons with guns can keep me from you.'

Another heavy breath. 'I have no doubts about your capabilities, Ms Snow. What a shame you weren't there to prevent Agent Campbell from discovering his wife's infidelity with Detective Moore. It's strange what broken men will do under extreme duress. At least Campbell's wife is safe for now.'

Astrid sucked in a massive chunk of the chilled air. 'What have you done with her?'

She was already mapping out how she'd get into the compound and make Sawyer pay.

'Officer Campbell would like to speak to you, Ms Snow.'

The voice changed on the line, Campbell's terrified tone sending a shiver down Astrid's spine. 'Oh, Astrid, they made me watch what they did.' She was sobbing so loudly Astrid didn't catch the next few words. '...there was blood everywhere, and the screaming, oh my God, the screaming.'

Silence followed. She gripped the phone, observing the paramedic watching her. She knew Sawyer was back on the other end.

'How much are you making from the human trafficking website for you to do this, Sawyer?'

The line hissed as he spoke. 'I don't know what you're talking about, Ms Snow. You can tell Officer Campbell is distressed over what happened with her husband and Detective Moore. To prevent her from harming herself, I think it best she stays with me for a bit. I have excellent medical facilities and personnel here; my people will look after her. I'm sure she'll be good as new in two or three days. Yes, Ms Snow, you'll be able to see Officer Campbell in three days, no sooner than that. What do you say?'

Astrid gripped the phone against her damaged fingers. 'Say hello from me when you see your boy, Sawyer.'

She ended the call and handed the cell back to the paramedic, wondering what to do next. He quizzed her with his eyes.

'Are you a friend of the family?'

'Something like that.' The blue lights were getting closer. 'Who called you out here?'

He removed a cigarette from his pocket and lit it. 'An anonymous tip.' His gaze darted from the house and back to her. 'If you ask me, I think the bloke in the living room killed the other one, called us, and then topped himself.'

'Why would he phone for an ambulance if he was going to kill himself?'

He blew smoke towards her. 'Who knows with these types of mental breakdown? Maybe he thought he might make a hash of the suicide shot, and we'd be his backup. Or perhaps he didn't want his wife to find him like this.' Astrid saw two pennies drop behind his eyes, and he added them up to four. 'Are you his wife?'

'I'm just a friend of the family.'

She gazed at the house, trying to understand why Benedict Sawyer would do this and coming up with no logical answers.

Will he let Eleanor go after three days? Why hold on to her for that length of time? Why is he holding her there against her will anyway? And what do I do now?

She had to get her away from Sawyer, but that wouldn't be easy. Even with the warning he'd given her, the old man would know she'd come for him and Campbell. He'd have improved his security and have everyone on his payroll watching out for her. She needed time to think of a plan.

Where am I going to go now?

Some of her things were still at Moore's house, and she had the spare key he'd given her. But the police would be all over the apartment once they'd found what had happened to him. There was Angie Delaney; maybe she'd help her.

And that would mean putting Angie and her mother at risk.

No, she couldn't do that.

So what next?

She turned to the paramedic. 'I thought the media would be here by now.'

An apparent murder-suicide featuring a prominent local copper and a Security Service member would be a juicy news story too hard to ignore.

'The Police Chief and the Mayor have ordered a complete blackout over it. I'm surprised you got here.' For the first time since she'd arrived, he looked at her as if she shouldn't be there.

'Why the blackout?'

The paramedic scrunched his eyes at her, giving his face the appearance of a confused rabbit.

'Have you been asleep all day? The President's coming here, part of a national tour of the country's smaller towns. Apparently, it was a last-minute thing so he can speak to the people before the election next year.'

'Is he staying in Bakerstown?'

The paramedic laughed. 'Yeah, our first presidential visit since Carter, but he won't be in town with the rest of us grunts. He'll be in the lap of luxury at Sawyer's mansion.'

That's why Sawyer didn't want her there. He'd taken Eleanor hostage to prevent Astrid from causing havoc at his place during a presidential visit.

She went to Campbell's car and put her hand on it.

Campbell's car.

She stood there, leaning on the vehicle while wearing Eleanor's clothes. What would the police think about that when they turned up? The approaching blue lights indicated she'd get an answer soon enough.

Astrid remembered the ride to the police station this time. The Officers didn't speak to her, yet she felt the resentment dripping from them. There was no arrest on this occasion, but she guessed they were desperate to throw her into that cell again. She spent the journey mapping out her responses to the obvious questions they'd fire at her while planning how to get Eleanor away from Benedict Sawyer.

When she got there, the mood in the station was a mixture of anger and sorrow. From the looks on most of the faces, she assumed they were directing some of that fury at her. There was no trip to the cells as they led her straight to the interrogation room. As she stepped inside, she automatically looked for Moore, finding the Chief and a Plainclothes Officer instead. She took a seat before being asked to.

'I'm Detective Newman.' He glanced across from her. 'You know Chief Colt.'

Instinct and experience told her to stay quiet, but one of the escape maps in her head, devised on the ride to the station, started with her asking them questions, at least one of which she knew the answer to.

'Where's Eleanor Campbell?'

They scrutinised her as much as she did them. Was Colt involved with Benedict Sawyer? A man who owned an entire town would have his fingers deep into the local police department. She stared at him and waited for the copper to blink, but those large frog-like eyes were unmoving.

Newman answered her question.

'We hoped you'd know of Officer Campbell's whereabouts, Ms Snow.'

She rested one arm on the chair. 'And why would that be, Detective?'

'You were seen at Campbell's house late last night, speaking to her and Detective Moore.' He paused for effect. 'And now she's missing, and he's dead. Murdered and mutilated most horribly while Agent Campbell was in the next room with his brains all over the carpet.'

Astrid settled into the chair and crossed her legs. 'Is there any other way to be mutilated?'

The Chief's scowl and Newman's grimace showed her flippancy hadn't gone down too well. The Detective placed his hand on the table. 'Plus, you were driving her car and, from what I know and see, you're wearing some of her clothes.'

'You think I stole her car and clothes.' They stared at her without replying. 'And then returned to the house.'

Chief Colt's eyes bulged. 'Perhaps you had a tiff, got angry, drove off, and then went back.'

His stupidity knew no bounds, and she guessed it might be a long night.

'You know about the attack at the Campbell house yesterday?'

A smile crept over the Chief's face like a fat slug on a mission. 'You mean the alleged assault on you?'

'Alleged?'

'Yes, alleged.' Newman placed a file on the table. 'Jim's report has no evidence of an attack on you at the house.' He flicked open the folder. 'The building was in a state and there was blood in the pool, but you could have planted that. Nobody saw any assailants but you, which is pretty convenient.'

'It is for somebody.' She shook her head. 'Why would I do any of this?'

The two policemen glanced at each other. 'That's what we've been trying to figure out.'

'And what fantasy have you settled for?'

The Chief shifted his bulk up to the table. 'You killed Caitlin Cruz and her kids, stuffing those bits of paper into their mouths.' His stare cut into her. 'It's funny how you were the one who discovered their connection to a human trafficking website, isn't it?'

Astrid twisted her spine into the chair. 'It's hilarious I was the only one capable of any real detection work in this station.' She knew that was unfair to Moore and Campbell, but couldn't help herself. 'What about the bodies in the cabin? Was that me too?'

Newman smiled. 'That was part of your misdirection. Kill two strangers and disfigure them as the Cruz killings. It was enough to delay things, and then the national cyber-attack distracted everyone.'

Astrid's laugh hurt her ribs. 'Did I do that as well?'

The look on the Chief's face told her he was enjoying this. And he probably thought her suggestion wasn't too wide of the mark.

'Aren't you a former British spy?' He scowled at her. 'Who knows what you're capable of and what contacts you have in international espionage.'

She turned to Newman. 'You're getting desperate. Detective Moore would be ashamed of you.'

He slammed his hand onto the table. 'Don't you speak of him like that.'

'I didn't kill him. Why would I?'

'Because he knew you murdered Caitlin Cruz and her children. You killed Moore and made it look like a twisted serial killer, just like with the Cruzes and the numbers stuffed into their mouths. Perhaps you did it to confuse us, or there's some other perverse reason in your head.' Both of his hands rested on the table now. 'Your time as a British Intelligence operative might have scrambled your brains. Maybe even you don't know what you've done here.'

'Why would I lie about the attack at the house?'

'To cover your tracks.'

'Why would I kill the Cruzes?'

'We'll find out, eventually. First, we need you to tell us where Eleanor is.'

Astrid wondered how much of this nonsense they believed. 'Do you have evidence for any of this, Detective Newman?'

His silence filled the room for a full minute.

'No, we don't.'

She stood. 'Then either get me a lawyer or let me out.'

They didn't stop her from leaving. As she stepped into the street, the image of Chief Colt's slug-like grin wouldn't leave her head.

Where to go and what to do now?

'Do you need a lift, Astrid?'

She turned to see Rosie Sawyer leaning against her car.

'As long as it's to somewhere with a drink.'

SAWYER DROVE them to a run-down apartment behind the Baptist church. It was on the third floor of a dilapidated building, and the elevator didn't work. The graffiti on the walls was the usual obscenities and badly drawn penises, apart from a large slab of text, claiming the reader as an inspiration for idiots everywhere.

She followed Rosie up the stairs and avoided the stray cats purring at her legs. She was glad to get inside and dodge the bouquet of cat piss. Rosie threw her coat onto a chair and went into the kitchen.

'Beer, wine or spirits?' she shouted.

'Tequila if you have it.'

Astrid searched for somewhere clean to sit, finding only a stained sofa since every other spot contained piles of Polaroids. It seemed as if someone had used the room to dump thousands of images everywhere, and she had to tread carefully to make sure she didn't slip on any of them. Rosie returned and handed her a fat measure of alcohol. She held her drink out to Astrid, who clinked her glass against the other one.

Sawyer grinned. 'Cheers, Ms Snow. And welcome to my humble abode.'

Astrid took a large gulp of tequila. 'That's putting it mildly. As the daughter of the man who owns the town, couldn't you have found somewhere more salubrious to live?'

Rosie shook her head. 'This is the best place for me. He won't think to look for me here, and my brother wouldn't be seen dead in this part of Bakerstown.' She gazed at the mess everywhere. 'This is my little spot of solitude and sanity.'

Astrid bit through a piece of ice and wondered if she should tell her host about her recent encounter with Jimmy

Sawyer. She thought better of it and asked a question instead.

'How did you know I was at the police station?'

Rosie sipped at her drink. 'Rumours are like wildfire in this town. Once the news spread about Robbie Campbell and Detective Moore with someone being questioned for it, it wasn't long before I guessed it was you they had in custody.'

'They didn't charge me with anything. All they did was throw baseless accusations at me.'

'Such as?'

'They think I killed Moore because he had evidence I murdered Caitlin Cruz.'

'And Robbie Campbell?'

Astrid finished her drink and shook the empty glass at Sawyer. 'They didn't say, but maybe they viewed him as an innocent bystander.'

'But why would you and Moore be in Campbell's house?'

'Perhaps they thought we were having an orgy.'

Rosie spat all over the photos at her feet. 'What? How would they get such a crazy idea?'

'Eleanor and I had a fling. Many blokes take something like that and extrapolate future behaviour based on their rabid imaginations.'

'Wow.' Rosie finished her booze. 'I want another. How about you?'

'Are you talking about the tequila or something else?'

Rosie laughed. 'Well, let's go with the drink for now and see what follows.' She took her empty glass. 'Why don't you take a seat?'

Astrid glanced over the cluttered room. 'Where would you suggest?'

'Push the photos on the floor. I need to organise every-thing, anyway.'

She went into the kitchen as Astrid did that with the Polaroids. They tumbled on to the carpet and spread out like the tide flowing into the sea.

Astrid grabbed a handful of them as she waited for her tequila refill. There were images of parts of the town she'd already seen, the shops and the churches, the cinema and restaurants, plus others she hadn't, places of great beauty like the bottom of the hills, groups of flowering trees in the spring, shots of kids at play, and one of the outside of the police station. She didn't need to see that again in a hurry, so she dropped those photos back into the group and scooped up another selection.

She was going through them as Rosie returned.

'That's a collection of spontaneous portraits I took this year.'

'Spontaneous? You mean you snapped them without the subjects knowing.' Astrid grabbed her glass and sipped at it.

Rosie laughed through the booze. 'Yeah, it was some-thing like that.'

Astrid nodded and looked through the photos. An African American woman sat on a bench reading a copy of *The Hate U Give*; a blonde teenage girl listened to her head-phones with an enormous smile on her face. A priest stood behind an American flag; a grey-haired man fed the birds. There was a certain quality to the photos she hadn't seen before, incandescence caught in the film, which meant they felt like more than images to her, as if they were living snap-shots of the beauty of life.

'These are great. You need to exhibit them.'

Sawyer blushed and swept the rest of the sofa clean to

sit near Astrid. 'You're too kind, Ms Snow, but not all of them are uplifting.' She pointed at one lying next to Astrid's leg. Astrid understood what she meant as she picked it up.

'You look nothing like him, Rosie.'

She put a hand to her chest. 'Thank God for that.' Her laugh was nervous. 'Jimmy got all the old man's good looks.'

It was a recent photo of Benedict Sawyer, and his steely eyes appeared to gaze from the Polaroid straight into her face.

'Why does your father hate me, Rosie?'

Rosie blew out her cheeks. 'I don't think he hates you, Astrid. He admires you.'

She stopped herself from choking on an ice cube. 'He's got a funny way of showing it.'

'He offered you a job. That seemed sincere to me. I know Jimmy's angry about that, so he believes it's genuine.'

'Do you know two thugs who hang around with your brother, cowboys with one in a black hat and the other in a white one? Neither of them is very bright.'

Rosie's laugh made Astrid's heart flutter. 'Yeah, that sounds like Chuck and Buck Jones. They went to school with Jimmy and have followed him like lapdogs ever since. I heard you had a run-in with them outside the Ranch House.'

'That was the first time.'

'There's been more?'

How much should I tell her? Do I trust her?

'Have you visited the town of Sugar Hill?' Rosie nodded. 'They sprang a sneak attack on me there.'

'I guess you dealt with them, but why were you there?'

Was that a note of concern in her voice, or was she fishing for information?

'I was searching for Caitlin Cruz's killers.'

She noted how Sawyer's eyes narrowed as she spoke. 'Why there?'

'I tracked a link. But your brother's friends were waiting for me.'

She told Sawyer some of what had occurred, but not all of it, and definitely not about her brother's involvement. And not what she'd done to him.

'What happened?'

'Someone murdered my lead using a knife I'd touched in Eleanor Campbell's kitchen. Then the cowboy goons jumped me.'

'Did you question the brothers?'

'I did, but they were useless. Then I returned to Bakerstown and the carnage at the Campbell house.'

Sawyer pulled up her legs and crossed them on the sofa, clutching the tequila to her chest.

'None of it makes any sense.'

Astrid peered into the prints scattered around her feet. 'It does to someone.' She scanned the images until she saw an interesting group. She grabbed them and took another taste of tequila. 'You took a lot of photos of the brewery.'

'I started a new project of recording every part of the town as it goes from January to December, but I paused it after what happened at the brewery. It was while the management shut it down after the accident. Bakerstown wouldn't survive without it. And it's our biggest tourist attraction. I wanted to get some shots inside after the accident and during the upgrade. It was the first significant internal change there since World War Two, and I thought I should document it, but it was a no go.'

'Even with your father's influence?'

She laughed. 'I think it was he who blocked me from getting in.'

Astrid went through the brewery images, her interest in the place increasing as she got to the last half a dozen photos.

'Do you have a laptop with internet access, Rosie?'

She shook her head. 'Sorry, no. But I have it on my cell.'

Astrid finished her second drink and put the glass on to the floor, finding a spot between the Polaroids.

'Can I borrow it while you get me another tequila?'

'Sure, of course.'

She handed the phone to Astrid and took the empty glass from the carpet. Rosie shot her a curious look as she retreated to the kitchen.

Astrid smiled at her, and then opened the browser. It didn't take long to find what she wanted, and she returned the phone to Rosie when she arrived with their next tipple. She'd left the web page on the screen, so Rosie saw it as she sat down.

'Do you want to take a brewery tour?'

'Yes, the first chance we get tomorrow.'

Rosie furrowed her eyebrows. 'How come?'

Astrid slurped her drink and handed Rosie the photos which had attracted her attention. In each of them, Caitlin Cruz was striding through the brewery gates.

'According to your writing on the back of these, they're from consecutive days, all in the run-up to the accident where two people died.' And a month after the last photo was taken, Cruz was also dead. 'Did you know Caitlin, Rosie?'

Sorrow danced across Sawyer's face. 'Hardly; we didn't exactly move in the same social circles, but I knew her by reputation.'

'What reputation?'

Rosie Sawyer sucked in her cheeks. 'From what I overheard of my father complaining about her, Cruz imagined herself as an online investigative journalist. I think it began with work she did in that church of hers, and then she started sticking her nose into places she shouldn't.'

There was resentment in her tone which Astrid hadn't noticed before. Was it aimed at Cat Cruz or because her father seemed to take more notice of her than his daughter?

'What did Caitlin discover, Rosie?'

'I'm not a hundred per cent sure, but I think it was to do with the brewery.'

'What about it?'

'People died there and it nearly shut down. Bakerstown would have turned into a ghost town if that had happened.'

'Wasn't that an accident?'

'That's what the management claimed, but they're not to be trusted.'

'Because your father owns the place?'

'Exactly.' Rosie removed a vape from her pocket and was about to light it when Astrid shook her head.

'So what happened if it wasn't an accident?'

Sawyer placed the vape on the arm of the sofa. 'I don't know, but people died, and not just in the brewery.'

'There was a cover-up?' Rosie nodded. 'And they attributed the deaths to something else.'

'You don't understand how ruthless my father is. He'll do anything to protect himself and his business.'

Astrid glanced through the pictures again. 'You were outside the building on four consecutive days to get these photos of Caitlin. Was that coincidence?'

Rosie shrugged. 'Probably. I've been taking a lot of pics of the town.' She snatched another group from the floor. 'Look, these are all the Baptist church on different days. If you go through everything I took, you'll find groups of every inch of Bakerstown. It's just the way I work.'

Astrid processed all this additional information.

'We need to get inside that brewery tomorrow to see what your father is covering up.'

And why he's killing people in the process.

19   DRINKING ABOUT MY BABY

It wasn't inevitable she and Rosie would end up in bed, but once the American woman slipped Bowie's *Low* album into the CD player, Astrid guessed which way it would go. That and devouring a bottle of tequila between them loosened any inhibitions there may have been.

Sawyer had furnished the bedroom on a meagre budget, but it was full of more warmth than Astrid expected for somewhere so run down. She peered at the far wall, staring at the collection of photos Rosie had placed there. She rose while Rosie slept and looked at every image, noticing a pattern in the layout similar to what she'd seen on the map that night in her cell. The Police Department's photo led to one of the Well-Read bookstore, then came Tom's Diner, the drugstore, the perfume shop and Siggy's Used Cars. The row below that connected pictures of the movie theatre, the town hall, the United Methodist Church, the First Church of the Baptist, the Jesus Cheeses deli, and then a group of images that interested her the most: the Bakerstown Brewery.

She crawled out of bed, a chill in the air making the hair

on her naked body stand on end. She pushed her toes into the carpet and strode towards the photo collage. Last night, she'd grabbed those snaps of Caitlin Cruz outside the brewery, and she placed them with the others on the wall.

What were you looking for in there, Cat?

It had to be something to do with the accident. She gazed hard at the images, hoping the longer she looked, the more likely the solution would pop into her head. Only Rosie's fingers on her shoulder dragged her mind from the question of Caitlin Cruz's mission at the Bakerstown Brewery.

'The tour isn't for another three hours.' She ran her hand over Astrid's skin. 'Shall we design a plan for what to do when we're inside?'

Astrid turned from the wall and put her hands on Rosie's hips, the touch and scent of the American sending a shudder through her body.

'We need to eat before that.'

'Will breakfast do?'

She pulled Rosie into her. 'After.'

ASTRID STOOD outside the brewery just before twelve, with five minutes to go before the start of the tour. The dark glasses and wide hat Rosie had given her might not have been the most sophisticated disguise, but the fewer prying eyes she attracted, the better. About a dozen people waited there; tourists, she assumed. They gossiped amongst themselves, more interested in the upcoming presidential visit to Bakerstown than the tour they were about to take. Some of them spoke about the troops returning home and how that was a good thing. Nobody mentioned the cyber-attacks, seemingly unconcerned since they were over and hadn't affected ordinary citizens. She peered at the gates and imagined the leader of the free world stopping there during his tour and sipping on that terrible beer she'd had the night she got drunk.

Rosie had entered the brewery thirty minutes earlier, going inside on the pretence of working for her father. The idea was for her to enter the management office and commandeer it for her work. Astrid would meet her there and crack the computer's security and search for anything relating to the accident or Caitlin Cruz. It wasn't the greatest plan she'd ever designed, but it was all she had until something else turned up.

They weren't outside the brewery's massive front gates, but around the side where she gazed over to the hills and the forest at the bottom. If she went down to enjoy that spot of nature, she could continue on for a few miles and reach the point in the woods where she'd escaped from Eleanor Campbell's house the night of the attack. Just the thought of Campbell made her think about her imprisoned in Benedict Sawyer's oily grasp. And then the image of Jim Moore's mutilated corpse flashed across her retinas.

Why maim the body like that?

Why would Sawyer kill Robbie Campbell and Moore? Did they discover something about the cover-up of the accident, or what had happened to Caitlin and her family? If either of them did, it would explain why Benedict Sawyer had them murdered. Framing her for it might just have been an added benefit for the old man.

She stared at the brewery. Everything started there, from the so-called accident to the murders and the Campbell house's terrible events. If she didn't get any answers now, what would she do?

The gates opened and a member of staff welcomed them in. Astrid paid her fee and followed the others inside. A young woman led them down a long corridor adorned with large photos of hops standing golden in the sun and glowing pints pulled into glittering glasses until they reached the start of the tour and the origins of the Baker-stown Brewery.

Their guide didn't look old enough to drink in the US, although she would have been fine down the pub in Britain, but she seemed to know what she was speaking about. She spent two minutes explaining how the brewery had grown from its humble beginnings to its current position as the town's hub. There was no mention of Benedict Sawyer or his family as she went straight into beer production mechanics.

Whole-leaf hops were their speciality and allegedly added extra flavour to their brew. Astrid didn't want to dispute the young woman's words, and her memories of drinking in the Ranch House that first night in town might still have been shaky, but she remembered how terrible the local brew was. Or perhaps that's what had wiped some of what she did that night from her brain.

The tour guide took them past the laboratory where they peered through the window to admire the science on show. Astrid watched men and women pouring liquids into glass phials, and for a moment, she imagined she was inside one of the big pharmaceutical companies; or in a modern remaking of Jekyll and Hyde. As they moved closer to the brewing process, she smelt mashing grains and boiling wort. Then came the aroma of fermenting yeast, which always reminded her of sulphur. Some of her party gripped on to their noses and grimaced, but she liked the odour and pictured every murderous person she'd ever met suffering in

Hell. Benedict Sawyer was one of them, flailing on his back like an obese turtle as a legion of demons stabbed at him with fiery pitchforks.

But the aroma must have been too much for some as an older lady gripped on to her stomach and threw up all over the bloke she was with. The group parted as the tour guide slapped a hand over her face. It was the perfect distraction for Astrid as she slipped from the back towards the office they'd walked past two minutes earlier. Nobody stopped her as she strode down the corridor to the sounds of the woman throwing up again.

She reached the room and entered. It was windowless with grey walls and smelt of roses, which was a relief with the stink of vomit flowing through the air. On the desk were a computer, a notebook, and a stack of papers sitting under a frog-shaped paperweight. An empty bookshelf stood against the far wall; next to it was a photocopier and fax machine. She was amazed people still used such things.

There was no sign of Rosie Sawyer.

Astrid went and sat in front of the computer. She touched the keyboard and the screen sprang to life, flickering through a moving image of Donald Duck. The mouse was in one hand while she monitored the entrance. She didn't know how much time she had, so she scanned the files and folders for anything unusual. She searched for Caitlin's name first, unsurprised to get no results. It was the same searching for Benedict Sawyer and any links to his surname. Then she tried for the day of the accident, disappointed to find no mention of it. It was a frustrating and fruitless twenty minutes, so when the door opened, she was ready to be thrown into the street.

'Sorry for taking so long to get here, but I met someone I used to go to school with.'

Astrid stood. 'You missed nothing, Rosie; there's nothing helpful here.'

Rosie moved to Astrid and put a hand on her shoulder. 'It doesn't matter. I know what happened and it was no accident. Let's head outside, and I'll tell you all about it.'

They left the office together, Rosie seemingly unconcerned if any of the staff saw them. She led the way to the front of the building and the gates Astrid had entered earlier. Nobody spoke or looked at them. They tumbled out of the brewery without looking back, heading towards the car until halted by a crowd ahead of them.

Rosie bumped into her. 'Shit! I'd forgotten about this.'

Astrid glanced at the flags and posters fifty feet away, but couldn't work out what they said.

'Forgotten about what?'

'It's the annual Bakerstown Eating Competition.'

A trolley of food trundled past them, pushed by two stressed-looking teenage boys. A roll of plastic covered the contents, a mountain of corned beef sandwiches and hot dogs stuffed with meat. The crowd parted, and the two women stuck to the teenagers in an attempt to reach the car.

'People watch others stuffing their faces as entertainment?'

In a dingy hotel room a long time ago, she'd flicked across a hundred TV channels and found one where a man had sweated through eating a curry so hot, it could energise a nuclear power station. Was that what this was?

Rosie continued walking as she replied.

'They're competitive eaters. It's a national sport in America.'

Astrid checked to make sure they hadn't been followed from the brewery. 'Then we better pretend we're the same and follow this until we can get through the mob.'

They kept on going behind the trolley, observing the overexcited faces of the surrounding people, tourists and townspeople of all ages. As they pushed on, Astrid's stomach grumbled as she caught the aroma of the food on offer: grilled cheese and bacon, barbecue pork ribs, deep-fried shrimp, and curried chicken. Rosie didn't appear to share her growing hunger, her face turning greener with every step they made.

Their unsuspecting guards took a sharp left and disappeared behind the stage, leaving the two of them free. Astrid expected them to get to the car with no problems, but they found themselves blocked by a large group of people looking like they might be contestants, but who turned out to be part of a dedicated audience. She saw no escape without forcing their way through the throng and causing a commotion.

Rosie held on to her guts. 'We need to wait until the crowd parts after the first event.'

Astrid was stoic about it, even though she was desperate to hear what Rosie had learnt about the accident.

'What did your friend tell you inside the brewery?'

Rosie leant towards Astrid, but the throng roared around them as the contestants entered the arena. A beefy man with a punk haircut waved as he stepped on to the stage, followed by a young bloke with a beard as big as him, a guy dressed as Elvis in his Las Vegas pomp, a nervous-looking woman with Popeye tattooed onto her bare shoulder, a Prince lookalike who danced his way to his eating spot, a teenage girl with terrible acne, and a ragamuffin of a boy with long black hair. Astrid glanced at them all and wanted the teenage girl to win.

Rosie's lips moved, but Astrid didn't hear a word. Then the noise reduced, and Sawyer whispered into her ear.

'There was no accident. People died, and it was my father's fault. They covered it up, but Caitlin Cruz discovered the truth.'

'And what was that?'

The roar stopped Rosie from replying. The contest had begun, and Astrid knew she'd have to wait before getting an answer. The MC whipped the audience into a frenzy by reeling off the accomplishments of the competitors. Then he started a countdown from ten to zero, and the contestants began with the corned beef sandwiches.

Astrid watched transfixed as the eating started, with those on stage stuffing mountains of meat down their throats, munching on the bread as juice poured over their lips and stained their clothes. They lubricated their masticating between large bites of food with gulps of water or, in the case of the fake Elvis, swigs of Bakerstown Beer. The sight of that made her feel queasy. She pushed into her stomach, forcing the bile back while checking if her ribs were any better. They still ached, but not as badly as before.

As the competition continued beyond ten minutes, the table became drenched in juices and discarded food until it looked like a murder scene. Astrid didn't know what the rules were for this orgy of digestion, assuming it wasn't the last person standing, but who could eat the most in a set time. At the fifteen-minute mark, someone rang a bell, and the eating stopped. People then joined the competitors on the stage to raise numbers on large cards like the old-time glamour girls during rounds of a boxing match.

With sixteen corned beef sandwiches in fifteen minutes, Elvis was declared the winner, and he took the plaudits of the crowd as if he was striding down the street like John Travolta in *Saturday Night Fever*. The people in front parted as they and the competitive eaters prepared for the next contest, providing enough time for Rosie and Astrid to escape and get to their car.

'I feel sick.'

Rosie's face had turned a shade of pinkish green, which made it appear as if she was wearing a Halloween mask. Astrid grabbed her arm and dragged her away.

'Do you want to throw up?'

Rosie twisted her neck, gargled, and then spat away from them. It flew and landed on a scraggy dog who howled and sprinted off with its tail between its legs. Astrid shook her head and laughed as Rosie wiped at her lips.

'I had a bad experience at the competition when I was a kid.' Astrid waited for more information. 'I'd snuck away from Jimmy, and was at the side of the stage watching the contestants gorge themselves. There was a skinny woman who looked as if she hadn't eaten in years, but she devoured two dozen burgers and plates of fries, and I was awestruck. She turned to me and grinned. And I smiled back. And then she threw up all over me.'

All the colour drained from her face and Astrid thought she might faint.

'We better get you to the apartment so you can have a lie-down.'

Rosie sucked air into her lungs, and then let it out slowly.

'I'll be fine. I need to tell you what I discovered.'

Astrid placed a hand on her arm. 'As long as you're okay.'

'Beth works in the accounts department of the brewery. I hadn't seen her in ten years until I bumped into her in the restroom. She was scared. I guess she thought I was there to check up on her and the others.'

'And you didn't tell her otherwise?'

'I never got the chance. I think what happened has been playing on her nerves ever since.'

'So it wasn't an accident?'

'No. She only knew a few details, but two staff members died, and they weren't the only ones.'

'What do you mean?'

'Someone in the brewery killed two of their colleagues and maybe another six people in the town.' The amazed look on her face was matched by what Astrid felt on hearing this. 'And Caitlin discovered the truth.'

20 THE DOG

Astrid drove them to the apartment, figuring Rosie's pained expression meant it wouldn't be beneficial to have her behind the wheel. She wasn't feeling too good herself, but it had nothing to do with what they'd witnessed at the eating competition.

There was no accident at the brewery, but murder. And more in the town, including the ones since I arrived. So none of this has anything to do with me or the Agency.

But she was still in the dark regarding the brewery events, and only one man could help her with that: Benedict Sawyer. His veiled threat against Eleanor Campbell wouldn't stop her from confronting him sooner rather than later.

How she'd do that, possibly including getting through a presidential security cordon, occupied her mind as she guided Rosie into her apartment. Rosie gulped and grabbed at her throat as they entered. Astrid thought it was a reaction to what they'd seen at the food eating competition until she saw the figure sitting in the chair.

She assumed Rosie's shock came from finding an

intruder there, and not because of the mask he wore. Astrid knew it was Guy Fawkes's image, but it had long since transferred from having meaning only to British people. Because of its use in fiction and political protest, it was a symbol opposing fascism and tyranny. Yet she understood the man behind the mask didn't represent any of that opposition.

Rosie shouted at him. 'What the fuck are you doing in my apartment?'

Astrid touched her arm. 'Don't you recognise him?'

'What? How could I when he's wearing that crazy thing?' Heat shimmered in her eyes. 'Is this a protest against my father's wealth?'

The man in the chair uncrossed his legs. 'I told Pop to get rid of you years ago.'

Fear replaced her anger. 'Jimmy? How..., how did you know I was here?'

'How stupid do you think we are, Sister? We always know where you are. I don't understand why Pop tolerates you, but he won't any more when he hears about this.'

So Benedict Sawyer didn't know his son was there. That was good.

'Why don't you show Rosie your face, Jimmy?'

He twisted his neck towards her, moving the mask so it seemed as if his head was about to fall off.

'You know, English, I only killed the kids because of you.'

Something kicked her hard in the gut. 'You're lying, Sawyer.'

Rosie took a step forward. 'Is that really you, Jimmy?'

Astrid pulled her back. 'It's your brother, Rosie. I gave him that mask.'

Back in Sugar Hill, after she'd finished her work with

the screwdriver, she'd found the Fawkes mask underneath the pile of tools Sawyer had intended to torture her with. She knew of his intentions because he'd told her between his screams. Even the music turned up to eleven couldn't drown out the worst of his howling.

Confusion replaced Rosie's anger. 'I don't understand this. Why did you give him that mask?'

'I thought it might provide some enlightenment to your brother, Rosie, and help him change his ways.' She flexed her damaged fingers. 'But I don't think it worked.' She stepped towards him. 'There's no need to worry, though. I'll get rid of him.'

'I wouldn't if I was you.' He removed a pistol from his pocket and aimed it at her. 'You both should sit down.'

Astrid refused the order. 'Only if you take the mask off, Jimmy.'

He moved his arm and pointed the gun at his sister. 'I won't tell you again.'

Rosie grabbed her and dragged them both on to the sofa. As they slumped down, Astrid noticed there were fewer photos dotted around the room. Then she fixed on him.

Distract him before rushing him. But how? Plead to his better nature? Impossible. Insult him like before, get him angry so he's reckless and makes mistakes? But that risks increasing his fury, so he shoots us in anger.

'What do you want, Brother?' Rosie's newfound calmness impressed Astrid.

He turned the gun towards Astrid. 'When you were rolling around in bed, didn't she tell you what she did to me?'

Rosie kept her focus on him. 'You sent those Jones idiots to attack her. I know that.'

His fingers shook, but his voice never wavered. 'That

was just a bit of messing about, that's all. It doesn't account for this.'

With the weapon pointed at Astrid, he used his other hand to remove the mask. She knew what was coming, but Rosie gasped when she saw his face. Astrid was happy to see her work had settled in across his forehead because it had been difficult to get the tip of the screwdriver to cut through his skin as she'd wanted. But the word PERVERT stood out well enough; an experienced tattooist wouldn't have done any better. Where her lack of skill became apparent was her efforts under the eyes. The PER on the right cheek seemed to say PEP, while the VERT on the other one now said VAPE. She couldn't help but laugh at her clumsiness. Still, cutting into soft flesh never produces the best results.

Rosie gripped Astrid's arm. 'What did you do?'

She spoke through the laughter. 'I'm sure it was long overdue.' Astrid waited for him to explode, hoping it wouldn't be by shooting either of them, but something rash so she could get the gun from him. But he was unmoving.

'Laugh while you can, English, but you got those kids killed. In the short time you have left in this world, I hope you remember that and imagine their little faces melting off as I poured the acid over them.'

Astrid dug her nails into the sofa, knowing he wanted a reaction from her. But her calm matched his.

'Are you admitting to killing Caitlin Cruz and her children?'

He dropped the mask on to the floor. 'Why not? It doesn't matter what you know now.'

All the life had vanished from Rosie's face. 'Why, Jimmy? Why would you do such a terrible thing?' Sorrow seeped from her. 'They were only kids.'

Astrid answered for him. 'Caitlin discovered something about the so-called accident at the brewery, and your father had your brother kill her for it. Isn't that true, Jimmy?'

His smile twisted the scars on his cheeks, so it looked as if someone had spilt Alphabetti Spaghetti on his face.

'That's spot on, English.' He shook with laughter. 'And then the stupid bitch came to Pop and told him to make things right, or she'd go to the police and the media.' The gun trembled in his fingers. 'Imagine being that dumb.'

'What did she discover, Jimmy?'

He steadied his hand. 'There was no accident in the brewery. One of our incompetent brewers poisoned a batch of beer. We only found out when some of the staff drank what they shouldn't and died three days later.'

Astrid stopped herself from making a joke about the terrible pints she'd had at the Ranch House. 'This is what Caitlin learnt, and you killed her for it.'

He smirked like the Joker. 'It was more than that. Those two idiots stole some batches before they knew what was wrong with it and sold it in town.'

She imagined the problems that must have caused.

'How many others died?'

He narrowed his eyes. 'At least four that we know of. It's a good job Pop controls the Coroner and the senior management at the hospital.'

'So you covered it up.'

'We did. Until that nosey bitch found out.'

The low thump which had been vibrating inside Astrid's head for the last five minutes increased in volume.

'And you killed her for it. But you could have left her kids alone.'

He shifted forward in his seat. 'I was going to, but then

you turned up at the house, and I remembered you from the bar.'

'You were in the house when I was?'

'I was upstairs. The Jones boys were waiting out back in the car for my instructions.'

Her heart thumped loud enough to drown out his voice. Nearly.

'You murdered her children just to get at me?'

'Well, she deserved it for snooping into places she shouldn't, but you had it coming for being such a whiney bitch.'

She dug her nails so far into the sofa, she imagined she might fall through the bottom. 'What?'

'I heard you talking to her as she patched you up. Moaning about your family and your sister, saying how much you hated them. And then going on and on about your niece, telling Cruz how much you loved the kid, and you wished she was yours. It sickened me, hearing that.' He put his foot on the Guy Fawkes mask and crushed it. 'And do you know what the ironic thing was?'

Her fingers ached. 'What?'

'Those two kids were sleeping in the other room near where I was hiding. And I thought I'd be kind to them.'

Rosie found her voice. 'By killing them?'

'Of course. Cruz was dead already, so it would've been cruel to leave those children as orphans.' He gazed straight through Astrid. 'You never get over losing your mother.' He glanced at his sister. 'And I knew this day would come soon enough, that I'd be across from you, telling you how you were to blame for their deaths.' He ran a finger over the scars she'd given him. 'But I didn't know then what you'd do to me, did I?'

'She should've killed you.' Rosie spat the words at her brother.

'It's too late now, Little Sister. I'll get the boys to cut up her body when I've finished, they'll enjoy that, and then I'll take you to Pop, and he can discipline you for betraying us.'

Astrid wondered why Caitlin hadn't used the phone she'd taken from her to call someone. But she couldn't since the battery had died in the bar. Astrid had wanted to text Courtney, but her mobile was flat.

But she still could have told me something in the car or the house.

Astrid searched her mind for the memories of that night.

Perhaps she said something, but I was too far out of it to realise. The drink and the beating left me dizzy. But I was better when she tended to my injuries in the kitchen.

Unless she somehow knew Sawyer was there. Astrid didn't go upstairs, but maybe Caitlin did to check on the kids and found him. That would terrify her. No wonder she got rid of Astrid so quickly once she'd patched her up.

Astrid scrutinised Jimmy Sawyer and understood how Caitlin would have been terrified by him and what he might do to her children. As he leant forward with the gun pointed at her, she calculated how much leeway she had in dodging the bullets. Before she had an answer, he fired.

Astrid thought she'd been transported into the middle of church bells, the infernal ringing affecting her so much, she felt she hadn't been shot. Yet he'd aimed point-blank at her. She clutched at her chest and found no wounds. She only realised Rosie was on the floor when her ears and eyes returned to normal.

Sawyer loomed over her with the pistol at his side, his expression as pale as a snowstorm.

'Look what you made me do, you English bitch.'

'You've shot your sister, Jimmy.'

His hand trembled as he raised the gun towards her. 'She's had it coming for a long time, and now it's your turn.'

Astrid didn't hesitate, pushing up and forcing her head into his gut. She tumbled over Rosie as she and Sawyer crashed into the back wall. A mirror shattered around them as she wrestled to get the weapon from his hand, broken glass flying past her and into his eye. He screamed as he dropped the pistol and reached for his face. It was enough for her to pull from him and go for the gun, until she stepped in the wrong place and fell over his sister.

She tumbled on to the couch, her hands trawling through the photos on the carpet. Jimmy howled, bumping into the wall as blood poured from his eye. But it didn't seem to impede him. As Astrid tried to jump up, he was on her and pushing into her spine. He got one hand on to her neck and forced her face deep into the sofa. She struggled to breathe as dust rushed down her throat, fighting for air while trying to push against him. His breath burnt into her flesh as he drove his face into her head.

'I'm going to visit England soon.' His voice was heavy enough to sink a leaky boat. 'I'll tell your sister how you died. I think she'll be happy, don't you?'

He relaxed his grip, so she turned to look at him. The blood trickled out of his eye and dripped on to her cheek. The scars she'd given Sawyer throbbed in his flesh as the fury oozed out of him.

'Hurting women and children is your level, isn't it, Jimmy?'

His psychotic grin reminded her of a clown from a horror movie.

'What can I say, English? I know what I'm good at.' His

knee dug into her. 'And the best thing is, you don't even realise why you're about to die.'

Heat soared through every sinew and bone in her, turning her insides into a volcano.

'So why don't you tell me, Jimmy? You can gloat all you want now.'

His weight pressing on her, plus the fingers around her neck, made it impossible to move. She tried to twist her legs and arms, but it was like fighting against a brick wall. He leant so close to her, she smelt the beer on his breath.

'This is so much bigger than a few brewery deaths, but you'll never know the truth.'

His lips were on hers. Perhaps he was going to kiss her, but she gave him one of her own. Astrid bit through the bottom of his mouth, her teeth cutting into his gums until she was clamped so hard to his face, it would be impossible for him to get loose without moving his body off hers.

Sawyer moved his knee enough for her to thrust her legs up with sufficient leverage to send him backwards and off her and the sofa.

He crashed into the Polaroids on the floor as she rolled over Rosie and grabbed the gun. Astrid leapt up before swinging her arm and catching him in the head with the pistol. The metal cracked into his skull and he collapsed. She stood there, her entire body shaking apart from the hand holding the pistol.

I could shoot him now and get this over and done with.

But it wouldn't be. She ignored the thought and went to Rosie on the floor, bending her knees and placing her hand on Rosie's back. Relief ran through her when she realised Rosie still lived. She placed the weapon to the side, got her arms underneath Rosie and turned her over, shocked but pleased to see no blood.

But he fired the gun. I heard it.

It didn't matter now. She had to wake her while her brother was unconscious. She put her hands on Rosie's shoulders and shook as hard as she could.

'Can you hear me, Rosie?'

It took a couple of shakes before she spluttered into life.

'What..., what happened, Astrid?'

She lifted Rosie forward and pulled her into her. That's when she solved the mystery.

'Your hobby saved you.'

They separated and Rosie reached into her jacket and removed the broken Polaroid camera: two bullets filled its innards.

'My brother owes me a new one.' She glanced over Astrid's shoulders at him. 'Is he still alive?'

Astrid stood. 'For now.' She held out her hand and pulled her up. 'We need to get you from here; it's not safe.'

Rosie agreed. 'Of course, but where?'

It didn't take Astrid long to decide on somewhere they could lie low. She reached into her pocket and removed the spare set of keys Jim had given her for his apartment.

'These are for Detective Moore's place; do you know where it is?' Rosie nodded. 'Good. The police should have finished there by now. You head there and wait for me. Then we'll decide what to do next.'

Rosie took the keys. 'What will you do?'

Something I should have done in Sugar Hill.

'I'm going to make sure your brother hurts no one ever again.'

21 DEMOCRACY

It was hungry work, dealing with Jimmy Sawyer. Astrid didn't know if there would be anything to eat at Moore's place, so she stopped at a burger joint on the way and got takeaway for her and Rosie. She'd eaten half of the fries by the time she pulled up outside the apartment.

She expected zero police presence, and that's what she found. She strode up and knocked on the door. After a minute with no answer, she tried the handle and found it unlocked. She pushed it open and peered inside.

There was no sign of Rosie.

Astrid went in and a deep sadness swept through her as she closed the door; stepping into a dead man's life was never a good thing. The apartment looked the same as it had when she'd left not so long ago. The used beer bottles still stood on top of the sink.

'Rosie, are you here?'

She placed the food on the table and checked the rooms, finding the apartment empty. There was also no sign of the key she'd given Sawyer.

Did Rosie even make it here? Perhaps the police left the

door unlocked when they finished.

Astrid slumped into the sofa where she'd slept, and been attacked, not so long ago. She bit into a burger and switched on the TV. She flicked through the channels, looking for news on events at the Campbell house, but finding nothing. Apart from the latest update on the annual eating competition, it was wall-to-wall talking heads about the President visiting their little town, and how privileged they were he was stopping in Bakerstown first on his impromptu trip across America.

She moved past the local news channels and settled on CNN. A handsome man with short grey hair and dark glasses was speaking to his guests about the President's tour and its relation to his decision to bring American troops home. The experts examined any links to the recent cyber-attacks, but nobody appeared to have any answers apart from blaming the usual suspects. She found it curious all of them assumed the attacks came from outside the country, and nobody considered it might have been internal.

She listened to their conversation as she ate, wondering where Rosie was and how she'd get Eleanor away from Benedict Sawyer.

Why not wait the three days like he warned me to?

The question went in and out of her head like the tide as she finished the burger and stared at the screen. Something the people on the TV kept saying nagged at her, but she couldn't quite work out what it was because of all the other noises consuming her mind. And then a familiar sound brought her into the present.

She stood and went into the kitchen, a vision of Jim Moore cooking her food still lingering there. Then the noise came again, and she followed it to a drawer near the sink. When she opened it, she got the shock of her life. She pressed on the screen and saw the message from her sister. Relief surged through her when she read it.

It's all okay. The police are handling everything.

Before she could think about how the phone Caitlin Cruz had stolen from her had ended up in Jim Moore's kitchen, she heard footsteps behind her.

'I got pizzas, but it looks like you've already eaten.'

Astrid slipped the mobile into her pocket. 'I thought you'd be here when I arrived, Rosie.'

Rosie dumped the pizza boxes onto the table and threw her arms around Astrid. 'Thank God you're okay.' She removed her grip from Astrid's hips. 'What happened to my brother?'

Astrid moved away from her. 'You don't need to worry about him.'

If Rosie heard the chill in her voice, it didn't appear to bother her.

'I know, but...'

'But what?'

Rosie ran a finger through a stray hair and pulled on it. 'I can't go back home, not after what I've done.' Her gaze cut right through Astrid. 'So I thought I'd leave town with you.'

Astrid didn't know whether to laugh or cry. So she did neither. She twisted her hip to the side, catching the phone against her leg and understanding how it got from Caitlin Cruz and into Detective Jim Moore's kitchen drawer. In the other room, she heard the TV talking heads speaking about the presidential tour, and some rusted cogs in her head started moving again.

'You told me you knew nothing about your father's businesses, but I don't believe you, Rosie. I need you to tell me the truth now.'

Sawyer took a step back, and Astrid watched her chest

rise and fall.

'Of course.'

Astrid went to the window to make sure no one had followed Rosie.

'Your father wants to extend his empire beyond this small town, doesn't he? He's planned this for a long time.'

Rosie's cold expression sent a chill through the room.

'It's not just him. There's a group who've been planning something big for ages. Until you came along and worried them.'

Astrid remembered the barman at the back of the Ranch House throwing barrels of beer down the drain and claiming it was out of date.

'This has nothing to do with poisoned alcohol, does it?'

Rosie's eyes widened as if she was a child caught being naughty.

'No.'

'Was there an accident at the brewery?'

'Yes, as far as I can tell. It was negligence by the management, so they covered that up.'

'But that wasn't why Jimmy killed Caitlin, was it?'

'No. It's something to do with the President, but I'm not sure what.'

Astrid stitched together the bits she'd heard on the TV and finding her phone in the kitchen.

'So Caitlin Cruz discovered this secret, and somehow your father found out what she knew. Then your brother threatened to kill her children if she didn't do what they said. That's what he was telling her in the Ranch House the night I was there. She would have agreed at first, what mother wouldn't, but when she realised the consequences of what they were planning, she refused. Then she bumped into me and whispered in my ear.'

That missing memory had returned to her when she was watching the TV just before she found her phone and Rosie arrived.

'What did she say to you?' Sawyer asked.

The sight and sound of that night were vivid in her head, as if she was back there again before all the mayhem started and the bodies began piling up.

'"I won't be the Oswald," that's what she said. I couldn't remember those last words because they didn't make any sense to my brain.'

Confusion gripped Rosie's face. 'They make little sense to me, either. What's an Oswald?'

Astrid's hunger returned in a rush. She moved to the table, opened a pizza box, and found chunks of pineapple all over the top. She grimaced, pushed it to the side and hoped for better on the next one. The smell of barbecue chicken made her smile as she warmed her fingers on a slice. Bits of it clung to her lips as she took a bite and answered Rosie's question.

'Your father and his cronies are going to kill the President.'

'Fuck!' Rosie grabbed at her throat, and for a second, Astrid thought she'd throw up. 'Is there any booze here?'

Astrid nodded towards the living room. 'Jim had a bunch of bottles in there. Find what you like and pour me a large bourbon, and I'll bring the pizzas through.'

They were gathering around the coffee table to eat and drink when Rosie asked another question.

'Why would my father and some fundamentalist right-wingers want to get rid of a conservative President, especially when he's about to pull US troops from the Middle East?'

The bourbon warmed Astrid's throat. 'I was trained in

the Agency to analyse situations like this, but none of it makes sense. How and why would your father assassinate the President?'

Rosie wiped pineapple from her chin. 'My father is a law unto himself. I only learn about his secrets if I'm lucky enough to overhear him on the phone. He hates computers and doesn't use the internet or email. The only thing I know is he always plans his projects three or four steps ahead.'

'Like ensuring Robbie Campbell was in the Secret Service and knew the exact itinerary for the presidential tour a year in advance.'

'But how did he know he'd come here first?'

'I'm sure if we checked through your father's financial affairs, we'd find a substantial contribution to that first presidential campaign. This is just the Commander-in-Chief paying off his debt.'

Rosie glanced over the dead man's things. 'What about Detective Moore? What part did he play in this?'

Astrid sighed, remembering the kindness he'd shown her in this room. And then she felt the phone sticking into her hip; at least he'd charged it for her.

'Moore played the most important part of anyone. When your father had Caitlin murdered, he needed a false trail to throw the honest law enforcement off. So Detective Moore put those numbers in her and the kid's mouths. The human trafficking website is genuine and is probably run by one of your father's competitors. So they got two birds with one stone: a competitor shut down, plus the police and the FBI with their hands full for months, even years to come. Me being there was just an unhappy accident.' Electric pain stabbed at her gut as she remembered Jimmy Sawyer bragging about how he'd killed Caitlin's children because he'd heard her talking in the kitchen about Courtney and Olivia. 'But they didn't count on one thing.'

'Which was what?'

Astrid reached across and picked up the photo of Jim and his wife.

'He tried to tell me the night I was here, but my brain was still mush. I guess he believed he couldn't take any chances. The Police Chief had to be in on it, or it wouldn't have worked putting the squeeze on Moore. And the best way to squeeze someone is to apply pressure on the people they love the most.'

'I thought he was divorced?'

'Not divorced, separated, but he still loved her, and they had a daughter. I'd bet good money on your father having threatened them, and making sure Moore was aware of it.' *Just like he did with Olivia and me.* 'Moore tried to tell me that night. He kept going on about sacrificing everything you have for those you love, about doing anything to protect them and keep them safe. He said people would give up all their ethics and principles to defend who they loved the most, would even sacrifice the many to save them.'

She put the photo back and felt like smacking her head against the wall.

How could I have been so blind and deaf?

'I understand why my father needed to control him and the rest of the police, but not why you say he's so important.'

'Because if it weren't for Jim, I wouldn't be here now. He framed me for those murders; he placed my passport at the crime scene. It was Moore who pitted me against your father.'

And she'd only realised it when she found what was inside his kitchen drawer.

'What?' Rosie looked confused. 'I don't understand.'

'The closer they got to the end of this plan, the more the decent people resisted. Not only was Caitlin killed when she changed her mind, but her kids were, too. Moore wanted out as well. He wasn't afraid for his own life, just for his wife and daughter. And then I stumbled into town and got drunk.'

'What do you mean about Caitlin changing her mind?'

Astrid finished her bourbon. 'I was too ready to believe the fiction of her being an investigative journalist, my brain too mixed up to remember what she said to me until now. But she would only perceive herself as Lee Harvey Oswald if she was to kill the President.'

'When he arrives at my father's mansion?'

'It has to be. He has a reputation as a womaniser, someone who wouldn't turn down a night with a woman when he's away from the public eye. That woman was to be Caitlin Cruz.'

'Why would she do something so terrible?'

'Benedict threatened her kids, and what mother wouldn't do anything to protect her children? Even murder a President.'

'But she changed her mind.'

'She knew too much, so she had to die, and your father tasked your brother to do it.'

And he got me involved in this, him and Detective Moore.

'How do you know Moore was part of this?'

Astrid reached into her pocket and pulled out her phone.

'I always wondered what happened to this. Why wasn't this planted near Caitlin's body and my passport? It would have been more evidence against me. When Jim questioned me in the cell, I gave him the number of my boss at the

Agency, but he kept making excuses about not getting through. I ignored it at the time because I didn't want the Agency's help. I only realise now he must have gone through the phone when I was arrested and unconscious in jail. There are only two numbers on there: my sister's and my former boss's. Moore must have spoken to him, and my former boss explained who I was and told him I worked for British Intelligence. Then it went boom in his head, and all the gears fell into place.'

The penny dropped for Rosie Sawyer. 'You were his way out?'

'Exactly. A way out from under your father's thumb, a way to save the President and a way to protect his wife and child. What he didn't expect was Chief Colt's determination to prove me guilty.' She stared at the photo of Moore and his wife. 'His desperation left him putting all his trust in me.'

'He assumed you'd want to find who framed you.'

'He must have done, assuming any normal person would need to clear their name, never mind someone he probably thought was a female James Bond.'

Rosie laughed. 'And he was right.'

Astrid shook her head. 'But he wasn't. I didn't care. I was out of jail and just wanted to get out of town. People have framed me for murder before; this was nothing new to me. If your father had left things alone, I would've departed days ago.'

'What do you mean?' Rosie sounded disappointed by the thought of it.

'I was going to leave here when the police discovered the bodies at the cabin. I believe your father was trying to confuse the issue, getting the authorities looking in different directions. He had those two people murdered to make it look like the work of the Cruz family's killer; it was all part of his distraction, one which would lead to that trafficking website. And your brother killed the guy who set that up and tried to frame me for it. He didn't need to do that because I would've left soon enough. Even the cyber-attacks helped him. Then he sped up things with the home invasion here and at Campbell's house.'

'When he tried to kill you twice?'

Astrid smiled at her. 'That's what I thought, but they weren't attempts on my life; he was getting rid of loose ends.'

Sawyer narrowed her eyes in apparent confusion. Astrid glanced around the room and remembered the time she'd spent talking to Jim; how he'd cooked for them, and they'd spoken about music.

'Jim told me everyone at the station knew he'd been sleeping on the sofa for weeks. I'm guessing your father owns all the apartments on this block and doubtless has spare keys for each of them. He sent someone to strangle Moore that night. Unfortunately for them and your old man, they found me on the couch.'

'What about the attack on the Campbell place?'

'They weren't after me, probably didn't even know I was there. It was Robbie Campbell they wanted out of the way, and you don't send one bloke and some wire to murder a trained Secret Service Agent. But he'd gone back to Washington early, and I was twiddling my fingers on the computer in that house.'

'No wonder you were pissed.'

'I was more confused than annoyed. If the FBI had tracked down the people behind the website, I would've been more than happy to have left. By the time I discovered the dead hacker, I was royally pissed off, and your brother made it worse.' He'd paid for his mistakes, and Benedict Sawyer would as well. 'Your father only has himself to blame for what's about to come.'

'How so?'

'Because if he hadn't sent you to force me out of the car to the little rendezvous in his vape factory, I still would've left town sooner rather than later. Once he threatened my niece, there was no going back.' She flexed her sore hand as she regained full strength in it. 'Your father might think he's a master strategist, but he never planned for me, and I'm the one who will bring his house of cards crashing down around him.'

Rosie took Astrid's scarred fingers and placed them to her lips. She kissed the entire length of them before reaching up to her face and crushing Astrid's mouth against her own. They hung like that for an eternity. Rosie was gasping for breath when they parted.

'There are still a few things I'm unsure about. Who is the new patsy if they assassinate the President, and how does the brief vacuum in political power help my father and his friends? Are they plotting a coup?'

'I assume your father set the coup in motion a long time ago. You said it yourself, Rosie: he likes to plan way in advance, and in this case, it must have been years in the making.'

She imagined a younger version of Benedict Sawyer sitting around the table with a bunch of similar-minded people, all staring at the pawn they were waiting to play.

As Astrid bit through another slice of pizza, Rosie appeared to understand what her father had planned.

'You mean...?'

'It's the Vice President. He'll be their puppet.'

22 GIRL GOES DOWN

I t took a second or two for Rosie to process the information. Then her lips stretched wide and her eyebrows rose. A chunk of pineapple clung to her bottom lip, only tumbling into her lap when she spoke.

'The VP, my God.' She raised a quivering finger to her mouth. 'My father went to school with his father. Our families are virtually cousins.'

Astrid poured both of them another bourbon.

'Your old man and this group will assassinate the President.' She remembered the conversation she'd had with Maggie Delaney about her overhearing Caitlin Cruz use the term Hawkestra. Was this what she meant?

'And the VP will become President.'

'That's right. They're going to put him into the Oval Office, then instigate some global conflict to keep him there, pulling his strings all the while. They knew about the President's withdrawal of troops from the Middle East, disagreed with it, but he wouldn't back down.'

'You think my father has planned this for a long time?'

'I'm guessing he and his cronies have had a long-term

strategy to get his old friend at the most powerful table in the world, and recent events have sped up those plans.'

'You mean the troops coming home?'

Click, click, click as all the cogs fell into place inside Astrid's brain.

'That's the opposite of what they want. They need American troops in the Middle East because they need a war there: a holy conflict to give them as much access to oil as their greedy little hearts will take.'

Rosie dropped her pizza on to the table as the colour drained from her face.

'It's only one of two wars they desire.'

'Two?'

'I may not be privy to most of what he does, but the thing I see without any doubt is how he hates liberals and democrats.'

'He wouldn't be the first or last to feel like that, Rosie. I've seen it across the world.'

Rosie drank the bourbon in one go and coughed. The colour returned to her through the red bursting from her cheeks. 'I don't know about any of that. All I recognise is how my father detests weakness. He perceives strength to be a hatred of weakness, and anything which promotes helping others is a flaw to him.' Her eyes glazed over as the empty glass trembled in her hand. Rosie's lower lip quivered as the words crawled from her mouth. 'I mean passionate, sadistic hatred. And I'm not exaggerating. That's what proves he's strong, his zealous contempt for weakness. To him, kindness, honesty, and compromise all equal weakness.'

Rosie put the glass on to the table and sank into the sofa like a deflated balloon. Astrid wondered how long she'd kept all of that inside her.

Probably most of her life.

'So, as well as conflict overseas, your father and his group want a domestic war between the right and the left. He hates whatever he perceives the liberal agenda to be and set up the perfect spark with the tinder box of Caitlin assassinating the President. Her defiance scuppered that plan, but now he has the ideal substitute.'

'Who? You?'

Astrid shook her head. 'No. Someone much closer to home. Your father's going to use Eleanor as the Oswald.'

'Officer Campbell?'

'He's had to adjust his plans, but he likely thinks it's fate. My involvement must have irritated him initially, got him furious when he discovered Moore had planned to get me involved. Perhaps he loved the idea of a Brit engaged in his new American Revolution. Now, in his eyes, he has a liberal, African-American bisexual adulterer he can blame.'

Rosie sank further into the sofa. 'And there's nothing we can do to stop him.'

The TV blared in the background, spewing out more news about the forthcoming arrival in Bakerstown of the leader of the free world.

'What time is the President due at the mansion?'

'About nine in the morning. I got a text yesterday telling me to stay away until the weekend.'

Astrid explored her options 'It's Wednesday night now. The President arrives tomorrow and leaves on Friday. Only he won't be alive when he does. Eleanor will get the blame, and one of your father's goons will conveniently kill her.'

'What about the Secret Service Agents protecting him?'

'I'm sure Benedict has everything planned to the last detail. Robbie Campbell would have helped him with that.'

And look where that loyalty got him. 'Has the President's security been to your house?'

Rosie grabbed the bottle of bourbon. 'They were there this afternoon, checking every nook and cranny in the mansion and the grounds.'

Astrid racked her brains for Security Service protocol for visiting presidents. She recalled reading Agency documents about when a president planned to travel: Secret Service Agents would visit the destination up to three months in advance. There, they'd meet with local law enforcement agencies to work out the logistics of the visit.

'This is no last-minute trip. Secret Service would have visited weeks ago, collaborating with Chief Colt and his department. Detective Moore and Agent Campbell would have taken part in any meetings they had.'

'You think the mansion will be thick with security now?'

'No, but they'll return two or three hours before the President's due. The sniffer dogs will be with them, so we've got about twelve hours to get in and out before they arrive. How many people does your father have around him?'

'Forty or fifty at least.'

'Do you know where he'll have Campbell?'

'I'd guess she'd be in the suite on the third floor since it's the hardest to get to. There's only one way into there. You'll need an army to get in.'

'And where will your father be?'

'He spends most of his waking hours in the library on the first floor. That's where I hear him on the phone to his associates. There'll be security outside the room.'

Astrid got her phone, aware she still hadn't replied to Courtney's new message, and searched for the Sawyer mansion online. She found photos from outside and inside the building, plus a set of plans for it and the grounds. She asked Rosie to identify the suite on the second floor recognising this is what Americans would refer to as the third floor, and the ground-floor library.

'Is this an attic on the top?' She pointed to an oval-shaped window at the highest point of the house.

'It is. I used to play there when I was younger to escape from my father and brother. You can't access it from the outside.'

Astrid scanned every photo of the mansion she found.

'Don't worry about that.' She pointed at the vape factory on the plans. 'Can you get me into there?'

When Rosie nodded, Astrid knew she was ready. It would take about forty minutes to get there.

She put her phone away. 'We'll leave at three in the morning.'

'Why then?'

'Even if they're expecting something, most of the security won't have the mind-set to be mentally ready at that time. The human brain is conditioned to sleep then. They'll be unfocused and jumpy, which is perfect for me.

'So what will we do until then?'

Astrid turned off the TV and closed the curtains.

'I'm sure we'll think of something.'

THEY LEFT DEAD ON THREE. Astrid combed through Moore's apartment before leaving, taking a few things she hoped would come in handy. She'd done a sweep of the area before they left, making sure none of Benedict Sawyer's people were watching them.

Rosie was nervous, her fingers trembling as she drove.

'Don't you want a gun?'

Astrid shook her head. 'I need stealth, not brute force. This should do me for now.' She patted inside her coat at the large knife she'd taken from Moore's kitchen.

'What will you do to my father?' Astrid had already told her what had happened to her brother.

'He threatened my niece, Rosie. He has to pay for that.'

Sawyer slammed her foot on the accelerator. 'Good.'

23 IGNITE

It took fewer than thirty minutes to get there, and the electronic gates opened as the car approached. Astrid hid in the space between the front and back seats, dressed all in black to blend into the shadows. She'd found the shirt and jacket in Jim Moore's wardrobe. She ran her fingers across the leather, feeling she had a part of the Detective with her.

Rosie drove into the grounds and whispered to her.

'I'm inside and heading towards the warehouse.'

'Do you remember what to do next?'

'Yes. Park outside the front, then go to my room and lock the door behind me.'

'And don't leave unless I come for you or get a message to you.'

Astrid twisted her body to fit into the gap, flexing her fingers as the car trundled across the ground. Rosie provided a running commentary.

'The lights are on in the grounds. People will see you if you go in through the front.'

She parked between the mansion and the warehouse.

'Is there any security outside?' Astrid prepared to slip out of the vehicle.

'There's two in front of the mansion carrying rifles. They're looking at me.'

'Good. Go over and distract them.'

Astrid heard Rosie get out and listened as she plodded over the gravel. Tiny stones crunched under her feet as she raised her voice.

'Is my brother home?'

Astrid didn't hear the reply as she slipped from the back and fell into the shadows between the buildings. In the illumination splashed across the ground, Rosie wobbled on her high heels, and her ankle turned. She yelled as the guard reached down to catch her, and Astrid sneaked around to the rear of the warehouse.

She crept into the gloom, pushing against the building. To her right was the back of the mansion and with fewer lights than out front. Security patrolled that area, but they didn't look where she was. She moved along the edge of the wall and hunted for the unlocked door Rosie had promised would be there.

And she was right. Astrid pushed it open. Gloom engulfed the inside: just how she wanted it. She scanned the place, searching for the spot from her previous visit. She found the office and headed for it, making sure there was no one in the warehouse.

When she reached the door, she breathed a sigh of relief. What she hoped would be there, what she'd seen when she was frogmarched inside the building, was still there: rows of oil drums. She unscrewed the top from the closest and tilted it on to its side. A trail of dark liquid dribbled from the barrel as she moved away. The overpowering aroma grasped at her lungs as she delved into her pocket and removed the silver lighter she'd taken from Jim's apartment. She stared at the inscription on the back of it.

To the greatest love of my life. From Lisa to Jim.

She checked the time on her phone: it was one minute to four. She waited until the digital hands ticked around: 4am. Witching Hour for interrogations, night abductions, and sneak attacks all over the world.

The flame from the lighter flickered in her hand as thick metal crashed into the back of her leg. Her body shook as if plugged into an electric socket as she crumbled and toppled to the floor. She missed the encroaching oil slick by inches and dropped the lighter to the side of it. Somehow a spark hissed its way from the top of the metal, and the dark liquid slithered towards it. Astrid reached for it, but instinct told her to roll away and through the oil. As it stuck to her clothes, the pipe struck the ground where she'd lain, and sparks exploded from the concrete. She watched them illuminate a murky patch of air as she turned to see her attacker.

One of the Jones boys grinned at her. He spoke through crooked teeth.

'I'm going to enjoy this.' He slapped the metal against his palm.

The pain continued to surge through her as she got to her feet.

'Are you Chuck or Buck? It's hard to tell with you Dunce Brothers.'

His grin vanished into the darkness as the thick oil crawled towards the misfiring lighter. He didn't appear to have noticed their impending doom, but she was well aware of it. He was between her and escape, so she'd have to go through him.

He pointed the metal at her.

'Chuck's in the hospital with Jimmy. We know what you did to him. You're evil, lady.'

'If you don't move out of the way, Buck, I'll do the same to you.'

She kept one eye on him and the other on the encroaching fireball. She guessed they had less than a minute to get out of the warehouse.

'How could you do those things to Jimmy? You're a monster, and I'm going to punish you.'

Astrid ignored the stabbing pain in her guts. 'Just like you punished Caitlin Cruz and her children? You made those kids watch their mother die a horrible death, and then did the same to them. There's only one monster here, Buck, and that's you.'

She watched the briefest flicker of guilt behind his eyes as he lowered the pipe. That was the prompt she needed. She threw herself across the ground, cold concrete cutting into her legs as it ripped through her trousers, before pushing the sole of her shoe into his shin. The crack of bone snapped through the building as she jumped up and sprinted for the door. His scream rang out as the sparks from the lighter kissed the oil and lit the flame. The blaze erupted instantaneously, the heat hunting her down as smoke engulfed the building like a vast smothering carpet.

Astrid staggered from the warehouse as the flames reached for her, fighting back the cough threatening to choke her lungs. She shook the lead from her legs and crept to the rear of the mansion as the fire rushed towards its inevitable conclusion. The barking of dogs was on the other side of the grounds, leaving her free to reach her destination.

She leant against the wall, catching a breath as she peered at her target. Astrid gripped on to the metal and dug her fingers into the sides. She was halfway up the drainpipe when the explosion ripped open the warehouse. As a kid, she'd climbed up every structure where she lived, including clambering over spiked fences and along the narrowest of ledges, so a set of skinny pipes at the back of the building was no challenge to her. She was across the rooftop and at the bottom of the second-floor pipe when the compound erupted into a volcano of exploding oil drums and vape machines.

Panicked security guards scrambled everywhere, but she knew those were only the grunts, the outside protectors. Those inside the mansion would be unmoving, refusing to shift from what they protected. She'd reached the second floor and the roof beneath the attic when a large explosion turned the sky into a fireworks display worthy of Pompeii.

The wind flicked at her face, the chill of the night making the hairs on the back of her neck jump up. There was no pipe up to the top and the attic, but a ledge and handholds in the bricks were there for her to climb. All she hoped was Rosie had unlocked the window.

She grabbed hold of a disused light fitting and lifted her leg onto the narrow ledge a foot above. Behind her were the combined noises of frantic shouting, howling dogs and roaring flames. The smell of burning plastic and unknown chemicals drifted over her. A clutch of fumes flew into her mouth, and she had to steady herself as she coughed them out. If anyone glanced up, it would seem as if a human spider was scaling the walls.

Astrid ignored the noise and the stink, peering up to the next indent in the wall. Scarred fingers reached up and found the gap, the tips of her feet perched on the thin lip of concrete supporting her. With her other hand, she grabbed onto the ledge and dragged herself up, getting both hands on to the shelf to roll her body along the length of it. She lay flat, her legs and torso barely staying on the ledge as her heart pounded against her ribs.

She needed to raise herself and pull the window open, but she didn't move, gathering her thoughts and breath. Huge bursts of smoke drifted over from the blazing warehouse. It provided some cover, but the toxic gases also played havoc with her lungs. Astrid glanced to her right and peered through the gloom. From what she could see, the fire was too severe for anyone to get close to it, but she was surprised nobody had attacked it with water yet.

Perhaps the blaze will be enough to prevent the President's entourage from coming here.

She couldn't take that risk and had to rescue Eleanor. She grabbed the window and raised herself. The wind bit at her cheeks as she placed one foot in front of the other. She pressed her face against the glass, breathing a sigh of relief at the unlocked catch. The tips of her fingers were prising the window open when the explosion went off below her.

Whatever else was in that warehouse erupted like Krakatoa. The mansion shook and rattled, a great plume of smoke and heat devouring the night sky. The blast would have blown her from the ledge if she hadn't got a hand and one leg inside as it exploded. The force threw her forward and into the attic, crashing her headfirst into a rocking horse and a bunch of discarded children's toys.

Astrid rolled off a set of building blocks and on to the floor. She stared into the rafters and picked pieces of wood from the back of her jacket. She pressed her ear to the ground and listened: it was silent below. No matter the confusion she'd caused outside, the security wasn't panicking inside the mansion. It was what she'd expected.

She got up and checked her pockets to make sure the

presents she'd brought from Moore's apartment were still there. Once she'd confirmed they were, she went to the door. Rosie had told her there was a set of stairs leading from the attic to the second floor, coming out in front of the suite where she expected to find Campbell.

Astrid inched open the door. There were three armed guards below, two peering away from the room and one staring towards it. They must have heard the commotion outside, but they were doing their best to ignore it. She was about to change all that.

She turned to the back of the attic, searching for what she'd found on the map online. If it weren't there, she'd have to come up with an alternative plan. She thought that might be the case when all she discovered were boxes of books and more toys, but when she moved them away, she saw what she wanted: the opening for a service hatch.

Astrid wiped the dust from the front and slid it open. It seemed it was a long time since it had been used to move goods between the floors, but she hoped the wire and pulley system still worked. She turned her phone torch on and peered into the square shape. The cables were on her right; apart from that, it was empty.

She'd discovered similar transport systems in several stately homes and former Royal palaces during her European assignments. She understood how they worked, and she knew how noisy they could be. To reach the ground and the library, she'd have to go by the second-floor suite and the goons inside. Even with the racket outside the house, there was no way some security wouldn't hear the mechanism descending as she pulled on those wires. So she needed to give them something else to think about.

Astrid returned to the attic door and peaked out again: the security was still there. She reached into her jacket and removed a box of matches and the firecrackers she'd taken from Moore's apartment. She lit one and threw it at the two guards outside the door. She was leaping at the third guy when the firecracker blasted into their faces.

Bone cracked, and the goon's nose exploded as her palm met his face. He fired instinctively, bringing the rifle round in an arc and spraying the corridor with bullets. She was crouching on the floor at that point, focused on the shooter and not his colleagues, who he'd just splattered against the suite. She took the knife from her boot and stuck it into his throat. It wasn't enough to kill him as he slumped to one side, finger still pressed on the trigger firing into the door.

Astrid tossed more firecrackers on to the first floor before running into the attic and to the hatch. She climbed in and closed it behind her. It was a snug fit with her back tight against the panel. She pulled on the wires and hoped they still worked. Gunfire ricocheted through the mansion as she dropped, the wood creaking under the strain. As she passed the suite, she glimpsed through a gap in the wall what was happening inside. Everyone had moved from the door; their weapons pointed forward as they surrounded Campbell. There were at least a dozen men there.

She descended past the first level, which appeared empty, then reached the bottom and the ground-floor library. Thankfully, the service hatch was at the back, away from the only people she saw: two guards focused on the door. When she shifted her gaze through the gap, she observed Benedict Sawyer sitting at a desk without a care in the world.

How will I get out of here and across the room before they turn and shoot me?

Astrid reached into her pocket in search of another distraction, but she was out of firecrackers.

24 CURTAIN CALL

Astrid pressed her face against the gap in the service hatch. A breeze drifted down from where she'd come, bringing smoke and fire into her lungs. She held her breath and waited, peering out at Benedict Sawyer sitting at the desk. His eyes were pinpricks sunk beneath a dollop of wrinkled flesh, his focus on the digital screen in his hand and the flickering images dancing across it. He twisted his body to the side and she saw what fascinated him.

Is he playing Fortnite?

As she considered such an unusual thing, the noise from upstairs disappeared, replaced by a knock on the door. The security never moved and she understood why: she would have expected a trap as well.

If I can silently open this hatch, I could get up behind them.

She peered through the gap into the library. Stuffed birds hung from every wall, and not just any old birds; these were hawks. There were dozens of them, and as she hid inside the service hatch, she imagined all their dead eyes examining her.

That image was echoing in her head as Sawyer looked up and stared in her direction, gazing at the hatch. She was thinking about pulling the wires to take it up when he said something to his guards. It was so low, she couldn't hear what it was, and she didn't think his security could either. One bloke lowered his weapon and walked over to the old man.

Astrid seized her chance. She threw open the hatch and ran towards Sawyer. The guard next to him didn't have time to raise his rifle before she had her hand on the desk, swivelling her hip and lunging at him. She knocked him onto the ground and got her arm around Sawyer's neck.

The other guard jerked forward with his gun pointed at her. His only problem was she had her face pressed against the old man, ready to snap his neck. She glanced down to see what had engrossed Sawyer so much on the desk. The guy she'd bundled over scrambled to his feet and aimed his weapon at her. She stuck her foot into the bottom of the bureau and moved her head, so it was behind Sawyer's.

'Drop your guns, or I'll kill him.'

Neither of them did. She squeezed her arm against his flesh, and he gasped.

'They only take orders from me.'

Astrid kept her focus on the weapons as she spoke to him.

'You know I could break your neck in an instant.'

She loosened her grip a little to make it easier for him to speak.

'Then my men will kill you, and Officer Campbell will die.' He exhaled a sharp breath. 'There's no way out of this for you, Ms Snow.'

Even though he smelt of parchment and vinegar, she pushed her face into his.

'Then we have a stalemate, Benedict, and I'm sure I can last longer like this than you.'

His legs trembled against hers and she felt his chest rise and fall. Inside her head, she was busy trying to create a map to get her out of this mess.

'What do you think you'll achieve with this, Astrid? There's no way you'll walk out of here alive without my permission.'

'The President's security detail won't bring him here now, not with a raging fire and explosions going off next door. Your plan is finished, Benedict. It's over.'

His laugh squirmed out of her grip and sounded like an arthritic chimney sweep.

'It's a temporary blip, that's all, Astrid. Things will resume once my men have dealt with you.'

'There are witnesses to your presidential assassination conspiracy. You won't get away with this.'

As she spoke, she noticed the security guards inching towards her.

'Ah, Ms Snow, your desperation is showing now. Who are these witnesses you speak of?'

'Your daughter has evidence of your plot.'

His head twisted in her grip and she saw him glance at the bottom drawer of the desk.

'Don't be stupid. Rosie can barely find her car keys on a good day. To think she'd know anything of my work is ridiculous.'

She pushed into his back as the guards inched closer. If they stepped apart to get on each side of her, she'd be screwed, but as they'd moved forward, they'd got nearer to each other. And that's what she'd waited for.

It took her three seconds to decide what to do. She leant into Sawyer and returned his grin with one of her own, grabbing his phone from the desk as she did. He tried to say something, but the words were too slow coming from his mouth, by which time she'd hurled it at the bloke nearest to her. It hit him in the eye, and an explosion of blood and muscle erupted from his face as she let go of the old man.

The other guard fired his weapon as she moved from Sawyer, but he was too late. The bullet smashed into the wall behind her as she rolled over the desk and grabbed a pair of scissors from the top. The second shot split the wood as she pounced on the shooter and thrust the scissors into his neck. Blood poured out of him as he dropped the gun and writhed on the floor. She released him and was up and off before the now one-eyed security man could aim his firearm at her.

'If I'd known America was this much fun, I'd have come here years ago.'

She grabbed a silver letter opener from the desk and jabbed it into the guy's remaining good eye. He dropped his gun and howled. He fell to his knees, reached for his face and searched for something which no longer existed.

Astrid stepped by him and went to the door, making sure it was locked. Then she pulled a table and a chest of drawers in front of it. Sinew and muscle in her arms and shoulders ached as she grabbed the blind man's gun and left him crying. The other guard had died with a mouthful of blood filling his lungs.

She strode over to the windows in the library, smiling at Sawyer as she did, and checked every one, happy not only to find them locked, but barred. All that remained was to disable the chute she'd arrived in.

Astrid returned to the sobbing blind guy and pulled the blade from his eye. He shrieked and rolled on to the floor. She cleaned the blood from the knife on her jacket and stepped over Sawyer's phone, noticing the human tissue clutching on to the screen. She moved to the hatch and cut the ropes so the pulley system wouldn't work. Someone could climb down it, but she'd hear them well in advance.

When she was satisfied the place was secure, she stuck Benedict Sawyer in a chair and sat opposite him. She pulled out her phone and placed it on the desk.

'Is your offer of a job still open?'

He opened his mouth like a vampire rising from a coffin.

'Officer Campbell will die. Olivia will die. All you've done is for nothing.' Astrid rolled the letter opener between her fingers. 'I'm not scared of death, Ms Snow: do your worst.'

She placed the blade next to her phone. 'How did you convince Caitlin to kill the President?'

He wiped the spit from his lips. 'A child's mind is such a malleable thing. I learnt this at an early age when I observed my peers' actions, seeing them fall under the influence of things they couldn't control. I'm not talking about people: parents, teachers or other adults wielding authority, because that's an obvious control built on age, experience and a physical presence. Most of that control over children comes through fear and the promise of punishment, both emotional and physical. No, I was fascinated by how outside influences could control people. Sex and drugs and alcohol are the obvious ones, but others surprised me. I loved to read from an early age, but some of my associates became addicted to particular authors or stories and tried to live their lives in their image.' He shook his head as if trying to remove difficult parts of his past from his life. 'Someone I knew a long time ago came to me in deep despair, so crestfallen I wondered who close to him had died, and do you know what he was so upset about?'

'Enlighten me.'

His laugh turned his face into a Halloween pumpkin. 'It was all over some movie.' He wiped a tear from his eye. 'I don't watch such nonsense, but apparently, it was the last film in one long sequence of them, and someone changed the personalities and behaviours of his favourite characters. Not even killed them, but, according to him, they were as different from the other movies as night and day. He told me it was like losing his children. Can you imagine anything so stupid?'

'People get obsessed with all kinds of things. You're not immune to it, Benedict.'

'This wasn't an obsession; it was control. He'd become addicted to something not real, and it controlled every part of his life. It's the same with all non-essential things in the world, such as music and art and sport. Weak people need these, become dependent on them to deflect from their dull existence. I soon realised I was not like them.'

'What is it that drives you, then, Benedict?' She had a good idea, but wanted to hear him say it.

'To control others, of course. That's the only thing that matters. Right from the dawn of mankind, that's all it's ever been about.' She noticed his use of mankind instead of humanity. 'It's what fuels everything in life, Ms Snow, from governments to churches, schools to businesses, and everything in between.'

'So you controlled Caitlin by threatening her kids.'

'Oh my, no, it was nothing so vulgar. Cat had followed my every wish since she uttered her first word. She was much more agreeable than her sister.'

'Her sister?'

'Yes, your latest bed partner, Ms Snow.'

Realisation dawned on Astrid. 'Rosie?'

'Different mothers, of course, but the girls were quite similar until the age of seven. If you haven't got them by then, there's no point wasting any more time on them.'

'You groomed her.'

He waved a wrinkled hand at her. 'Don't be so dramatic, Astrid. I did what all responsible parents do and guided Cat towards her ultimate goal, though none of us knew what that would be until a year ago.'

'Parents, good, loving parents, don't do that to their children.'

'Oh, don't be so naïve. I know she's your niece, but don't you want to do that with Olivia? I could see it in your eyes the night I brought you to the warehouse.'

'I only want to protect her.'

'It's the same thing. You protect them by controlling their actions, even when they're not children anymore.'

She'd thought at first he was spinning her a tale as a delaying tactic, waiting for his security to burst in and rescue him, but the more he spoke, the more she understood how fanatical he was. Rosie had said it was a hatred of anything perceived as liberal or democratic, of weakness, but it was more than that. It was sociopathy mixed with megalomania. He had a God complex that was unmatched by any fanatic she'd encountered before.

'So why did Caitlin finally oppose your years of brain-washing?'

'Her kids, of course. Jimmy was only supposed to put the fear of God into her, but the boy can overstep the mark sometimes.'

'Did he know she was his half-sister?'

Sawyer's face resembled a hyena ready to pounce. 'Of course not, and neither did Rosie.'

'Caitlin's children were your grandchildren.'

He rubbed at the wrinkles on his chin. 'It's no matter. There's plenty more where they came from.' The cackle crawled over his lips and pained her ears.

'You know Jimmy won't be doing much of anything ever again.'

'You put him in the hospital, Ms Snow. I'm aware of that.'

'Did your people tell you what's wrong with him?'

His eyes glazed over. 'I didn't ask. If the boy was foolish enough to be bested by you, he can lick his wounds until he returns to me with his tail between his legs.'

It was Astrid's turn to laugh. 'Your son won't be licking anything for a long time, Benedict, and certainly not with his tail.'

'What do you mean?'

'You look ancient, Sawyer, but you're not; I checked your age online. You're seventy-six. Looking at your family history, I'd guess you could easily live to a hundred. It's not exactly a hard life, is it?' She heard noises from the other side of the door, people talking. She figured they'd be working out what their orders were once they realised the Boss was in danger. 'And Rosie told me you're always plan-ning three or four moves ahead, so I think at some point, probably when the hospital got in touch about your son, you considered a new contingency if this one went bust. I mean, how long have you been developing this little assassination attempt?'

He wheezed like a pneumatic drill. 'Wheels have been in motion for longer than you've been alive, Ms Snow.' There was pride in his voice.

'That's what I thought. It also makes me think you and whichever wealthy and privileged people you confide with have almost certainly got other revolutionary plans for this country of yours. So even when the FBI turns up here and you're locked away for treason, you still might see them come to fruition, especially if I'm not wandering around the States anymore.'

'Those things will happen regardless of you, Ms Snow. You hold no cards here.'

Astrid picked up her phone and found the file she wanted.

'But that's where you're wrong, Sawyer. You may have spent most of your life mastering the politics of manipulation, but I've used mine studying the limits of human pain, both mentally and physically, on others and myself. When the hospital called about Jimmy, what did they say?'

'They told me he'd been in a terrible accident, but he'd live.'

'Did you talk to him?'

'No; they had him sedated.'

Astrid pinched her lips and shook her head.

'Jimmy will never speak again, Sawyer. And this is why.' She showed him the phone and played the video. The sound was turned down slightly, so Jimmy Sawyer's screams didn't obscure her description. 'I used the claw hammer to smash all his teeth first. I had to pull them out to make sure he didn't choke on them. Then I crushed both sides of his jaw. Can you see here how easy it is to demolish bone with the correct amount of pressure?' She held the screen closer to his face. 'Next, I took a knife and sawed off both ears. They were quite big, so I had to hack at them.' She placed her fingers on the side of his head. 'Yours are fairly petite, so I expect they'll come off in a jiffy. He was crying a lot by then, so I used the scissors to cut out his tongue. I had to ensure he didn't suffocate.'

The camera twisted away to reveal the tools she'd used.

'Look at what he'd brought to his sister's apartment. I assume he'd done this before because no inexperienced torturer takes a spoon with them.' The screen changed back to Jimmy Sawyer writhing on the floor. 'Can you guess what the professionals use the spoon for? No? Watch this, then.'

In the video, she reached into Jimmy's face, using the spoon to scoop out one eyeball and then the other. All she'd focused on was how he'd threatened Olivia and killed the Cruz children, feeling no sympathy for him. Watching it again, she still didn't.

'I know what you're thinking, Benedict; what a waste of human organs, right? But considering all the terrible things your son has seen and done, I don't think anyone would have wanted those second-hand eyes.' Astrid stopped the video. Sawyer's face was like ash. 'For good measure, I castrated him as well, but I doubt that's needed for you. I'm guessing nature neutered you a long time ago.'

'I'll die if you do that to me.' He tried to force a smile, but was unable.

'No, that won't happen, Benny. I'm an expert at this. I've had older and weaker people than you survive for many years after enjoying my delicate touch.' She glanced around the room. 'Though I don't have such skilled tools to use on you, only those scissors and the letter opener.'

She held up the screen, showing the paused video and his son's broken and barely recognisable face. She was contemplating her back-up plan when he agreed.

'What do you want me to do, Ms Snow?'

The man she'd blinded whimpered in the corner.

'Send all your men from the mansion and get Eleanor

and Rosie in here. Remember, I'll have a gun on the door at all times.' She retrieved his bloody phone from the floor and pushed it next to his face as he made the call and issued her instructions. When he finished, she went to the window and watched the security troop out of the building.

'Are you happy now, Ms Snow?' She ignored his question.

Three minutes later, a knock came at the library door. Astrid held on to the gun as she strode to the entrance. She spoke from the side, out of the line of fire if anyone was foolish enough to try it.

'Who is it?'

'It's Rosie, Astrid. I've got *Station to Station* with me.'

That was the code they'd decided for the all-clear. She moved the furniture from the door and opened it. Campbell was in first, throwing her arms around Astrid's neck and nearly knocking her over.

'Thank God you're okay.'

'Are they all out of the house?' Astrid said to Rosie over Campbell's shoulder.

Rosie nodded. 'We're safe now.' She glanced at her father. 'But it won't be for long if we don't have any proof of what he and his friends had planned.'

Benedict Sawyer glared at his daughter before snapping his head at Astrid.

'You lied to me.'

She shrugged at him. '*C'est la vie*, Benny.'

Astrid pushed past him and the blind security guard slumped against the wall. Then she reached down to the dead guy and pulled the scissors from his neck. She turned back to Sawyer and wiped the blood from them on to the old man's arm. Astrid smiled at him as she bent to the bottom of the desk and prised open the locked drawer.

Sawyer discovered one last vestige of protest. 'You can't do that.'

'And yet I have.'

The wood cracked and she pulled the drawer open. She removed the contents and placed them on the desk.

Eleanor stood by her side. 'What is that?'

Astrid grinned at Benedict Sawyer. 'Hubris.' She opened the box and found twenty or so tapes and a cassette player. 'This is very 1970s, Benny, very Tricky Dicky.' She took the player and checked it had batteries. Then she picked a tape at random and placed it into the machine.

Astrid turned to Rosie. 'Do you want to do the honours?'

Rosie stepped forward and hit play. Benedict Sawyer's voice jumped from the recording as he spoke to an unnamed Senator about the plans to assassinate the President.

Campbell let out a massive sigh. 'I guess that's the end of this conspiracy.'

'Not quite.' Astrid handed her Sawyer's blood-stained phone. There was no time to console her over the deaths of her husband and Moore. 'You need to ring the FBI. Tell them you've foiled an assassination attempt against the President and to cancel his trip here.'

Astrid moved from her as Eleanor made that call and returned to Sawyer.

'So, what's your best score on Fortnite?'

———

THE POLICE and the FBI arrived thirty minutes later. Astrid was reluctant to go outside until Eleanor vouched for them. She didn't want to mention Robbie Campbell's involvement in Benedict Sawyer's plan to assassinate the President. But after Eleanor had explained the situation to the authorities and handed over the incriminating tapes, she took Astrid aside.

'I'm sorry I never told you I was married.'

Astrid held on to her hand. 'It doesn't matter, Eleanor.'

They watched FBI agents bundle Benedict Sawyer into the back of a van while Rosie was taken to a police car.

Campbell gripped Astrid's fingers.

'We led separate lives, Robbie and me, but it doesn't mean I'm not upset with what happened.' She let go of Astrid and wiped a tear from her cheek. 'I still cared for him.'

'I know, Eleanor.' She glanced at the van as it took Sawyer away. 'At least you'll get justice for his murder.'

And for Jim Moore, too.

They watched the police and the FBI take charge of the scene before Campbell drove them to the station, where Astrid gave the authorities her statement. Afterwards, as she sat outside the room where Jim Moore had interviewed her only a few days before, Eleanor strode towards her.

'I have to admit I cheated.'

'What?' Astrid's face rippled with surprise.

She showed Astrid the image on her phone. 'I went online and Googled those clues you gave me and found whose grave in Rochester you're going to visit.'

Astrid stared into the screen at the young woman with piercing eyes and the iconic jazz-age bob peering back at her from across the century. Many things had helped Astrid survive a terrible childhood, but it was the image and idea of Louise Brooks which fuelled her passion for a life where no one would control her anymore.

'Well done, Eleanor.'

'So what should I watch first? *Pandora's Box* or *Diary of a Lost Girl*?'

Astrid's silent laugh echoed inside her head. 'It doesn't matter; both will change you forever.'

Campbell left Astrid to speak to Chief Colt. While she sat, Astrid considered which flowers to buy for the grave.

ABOUT THE AUTHOR

Andrew French lives amongst faded seaside glamour on the North East coast of England. He likes gin and cats but not together, new music and old movies, curry and ice cream. Slow bike rides and long walks to the pub are his usual exercise, as well as flicking through the pages of good books and the memoirs of bad people.

Find out more at www.andrewsfrench.com

Facebook:

https://www.facebook.com/A-S-French-Author-150145625006018

Twitter:

www.twitter.com/andrewfrench100

Instagram:

www.instagram.com/andrewfrench100

And replies to all his email at mail@andrewsfrench.com

If you have the time, please leave a review at Amazon or Goodreads

Thank you!

ACKNOWLEDGMENTS

Many thanks to my wonderful wife for all her support and patience.

Lost in America edited by Alison Jack.

Cover design by James, GoOnWrite.com